Robert George Collier Proctor

Jan van Doesborgh, Printer at Antwerp

An Essay in Bibliography

Robert George Collier Proctor

Jan van Doesborgh, Printer at Antwerp
An Essay in Bibliography

ISBN/EAN: 9783337251000

Printed in Europe, USA, Canada, Australia, Japan

Cover: Foto ©Raphael Reischuk / pixelio.de

More available books at **www.hansebooks.com**

JAN van DOESBORGH

PRINTER AT ANTWERP

AN ESSAY IN BIBLIOGRAPHY

By ROBERT PROCTOR

LONDON

PRINTED FOR THE BIBLIOGRAPHICAL SOCIETY

AT THE CHISWICK PRESS

DECEMBER 1894

EDVARDO GORDONO DVFF

AVCTORI SCRIPTOR

D. D. D.

PREFACE.

HE present essay is divided into three parts. The first part is introductory; in it is given miscellaneous information respecting the printer Jan van Doesborgh and his productions. The second part consists of a bibliography, in which the books are arranged in an order as nearly as possible chronological. The third part contains three sections: the first is a list of the woodcuts used in those of the books which I have been able to examine; the second section is devoted to the woodcut borders; and the third to the woodcut or metal initials and various minor ornaments used in the same books.

For never-failing help, advice, and encouragement I am deeply indebted to Mr. E. Gordon Duff. My best thanks are due to Mr. Christie Miller and Mr. R. E. Graves for opportunity to examine at my leisure the books in the library at Britwell; to Mr. A. H. Huth, for permission to reproduce Plate II.; to Mr. C. H. Coote for valuable assistance in Nos. 3, 4, and 22; and to the Librarian of the University of Cambridge. I have also to express my most sincere gratitude to Professor Henri Logeman, of Ghent, for most kind and generous help.

R. P.

PART I.
INTRODUCTORY.

INTRODUCTORY.

EW periods in the history of printing have been so much neglected, in proportion to their merits, as the years immediately succeeding those in which the new art obtained a hold on the peoples of Europe. In strong contrast with the attention paid to the productions of the printing-press in the fifteenth century, the typographical history of the early years of the sixteenth century is, with the exception of one or two exceptionally famous presses, to all practical purposes a closed book to the student. This is the more striking in the case of the Netherlands, because, while the fifteenth-century press in that country has been treated with far greater thoroughness than elsewhere in the works of Holtrop, Campbell, Conway, and Bradshaw, no bibliographer has yet attempted to do for the presses of the Low Countries in the beginning of the sixteenth century what the *Repertorium* of Weller and the *Deutsche Annalen* of Panzer have done for those of Germany. Van Iseghem's work on Thierry Martens, a book now considerably out of date, is still the only bibliography of this period of any note. To an English reader the interest of the period chiefly centres in Antwerp, a town which, though it received the art of printing late, rose rapidly to a foremost position as a typographical centre. This was mainly due to the enterprise of Gheraert Leeu, who moved

3

from Gouda in 1484, and, till his death in 1493, displayed extraordinary energy and enterprise.

It was doubtless the importance of the English trade at Antwerp that suggested to him the production of books for the English market, and his influence, probably to some extent, determined the character of the numerous English books which issued from Antwerp presses after his death. The *Rudimenta* of Perottus, printed by Aegidius van der Heerstraten at Louvain about the year 1487, is indeed an earlier example of a book intended for English use, but to Leeu must be given the credit of having organized this branch of the book trade in any effective manner. The demand for popular literature was what Leeu and his successors attempted to satisfy, and we find accordingly that the English books printed by them are almost entirely confined to the four classes of romances, grammars, almanacks, and service-books, almost all small and therefore cheap, and either suited to the popular tastes, or certain of a large sale because universally used as school-books. Later, however, the influence of the Reformation caused a complete change, and we find that, from about 1530 down to the end of the century, the English presses of Antwerp were monopolized in turn by exiled theologians of the religious party which happened to be out of favour at the particular time.

Among those who may have inherited Leeu's traditions and practice with regard to English trade, Jan van Doesborgh is by far the most important figure. The only attempt at a collection of what is known about him is the *Note* by Prof. Arber, which is prefixed to his reprint of the *New Lands* entitled *The first three English books on America* [1885; p. xxv].[1] This, while not professing to be more than an opening of the subject, is very useful as a guide to further investigation, and I am very largely indebted to it.

Of Jan van Doesborgh's life we know but little, and that little is to a large extent quite impersonal. His native town, Doesborgh, is a small place not far from Arnhem, at the junction of the Oude and Nieuwe Ijssel. Its sole appearance in history is in the year 1585,

---

[1] For a summary list of the books printed by Jan van Doesborgh mentioned in Part I. see the beginning of Part II. [*infra*, p. 19].

when it was sacked by the Spanish troops. Jan van **Doesborgh, like**
so many of the Dutch and Belgian printers, seems never **to** have
made use of his true surname. The books which are at present the
earliest known productions of his press shew us that he succeeded **to**
the business of Roelant van den Dorpe, the printer of the *Brabant
Chronicle* of 1497, who died in 1500. His widow carried on the
business for some, but seemingly only **a** short, time, for no books
are known printed by her after 1501 ; but at **some time** previous to
1508 we find the devices used **by R.** van den **Dorpe** and his widow
in Jan van Doesborgh's possession, as well as **his** type and (at a later
period) his woodcuts. R. van den Dorpe lived in 1497 "in die
huyvetters strate, bi onser vrouwen broeders." But a later book, the
Seer minnelijcke woerden, is dated from the Iron Balance, "aen
dijseren waghe." For these see Campbell's *Annales*, Nos. 508,
1785. It was from the Iron Balance that the books printed by
R. van den Dorpe's widow were issued, and the name reappears in
the colophons of several of J. van Doesborgh's books. Although **it**
is nowhere expressly stated, there can be little doubt that this same
house is meant in other colophons in which J. van Doesborgh's shop
is said to be " by the Cammerpoorte." This position, both inside
and outside the gate, was the central one for the printers of that
period. Govaert Back's " Vogelhuis " was " near the Cammerpoorte" [colophon to the *Herbarius* of 1511 ; Van der Meersch,
Recherches, etc., Gand, 1856, p. 126], Henrik Eckert lived " bi der
Cammerpoerten int huys van Delft " [Hain 12010], Henrik de
Lettersnider, who left Antwerp for Delft in 1500, lived in the
Cammerstraet, next door to the Golden Unicorn, where Liesvelt
and afterwards **Vorsterman** lived, "buyten die Cammerpoorte "
[Campbell, *Annales*, **Nos.** 1026, 549ᴬ]. From December 1521
onwards J. van Doesborgh lived " op die Lombaerde veste, inden
aren van die vier evangelisten." That the Lombaerde veste was not
far from the Cammerpoorte is shown by the colophon to the *Ouder
vader collatie* printed by Mich. Hillen in 1506 " bi der Camer poorte
op die Lombaerde veste " [see No. 3 of the J. Kockx sale catalogue,
Antw. 1891]. A plan of Antwerp, such as **that** in Baedeker's
Belgium and Holland, shews the Cammerstraet, or **Rue des** Peignes,

running in a south-easterly direction from near the Place Verte, as a continuation of the Vieux Marché aux Blés. The Rempart du Lombard (Lombaerde Veste) is a turning out of this street, and runs north-eastwards behind the Post Office, parallel to the Marché aux Souliers. An old plan (that by P. Verbiest, *Antwerpia: constructionis eius primordia et incrementa*, c. 1665, or that by Harrewyn, Brussels, 1733) indicates the Cammerpoorte at the point where the Cammerstraet crossed the old moat or ditch of the enceinte, close to the corner of the Lombaerde Veste. The Cammerstraet continued outside the gate for a considerable distance in a straight line under the same name.

In the year 1508, the very year in which J. van Doesborgh issued his first dated book, the *Reyse van Lissebone*, we find a record of his admission as "vrijmeester" of the Sint-Lucas-gilde [*De Liggeren . . . der Antwerpsche Sint Lucasgilde, afgeschr. van P. Rombouts en T. van Lerius*, part i., p. 69]; he is there described as "verlichtere" or illuminator, a profession which may possibly in some degree account for the profuse way in which most of his books are illustrated with woodcuts. This description was thought by Dr. Campbell [Arber, *Note*] to show that he was not at that time a printer. This does not seem conclusive, as during the early years of typography many printers combined other occupations with the practice of their art; and it is on the whole improbable that he would have succeeded to R. van den Dorpe's business so long a time as seven years after his widow ceased working his press. However, such cases are not entirely unknown, and the relations between William of Malines and Richard Pynson form an instance in point. But we have positive evidence that Dr. Campbell's hypothesis is untenable in the fact that, as will be shown later, three at least of the extant productions of J. van Doesborgh must be assigned to a date earlier than that of the *Reyse van Lissebone*.

Of J. van Doesborgh's connection with other printers than R. van den Dorpe we know very little. In the *Wonderful Shape* an initial is used which once belonged to Leeu, but otherwise Henrik Eckert is the chief of those with whom we find him in

6

touch. Not only were the Chronicle set of cuts used by Eckert in his edition of 1512, the new cuts found in that edition being subsequently used with the original set by J. van Doesborgh, but the cut of S. Augustine used in the *Dieren Palleys* had previously passed through Eckert's hands. Between Vorsterman and our printer the relations may have been less friendly; the Dutch edition of *Virgilius* printed by Vorsterman is illustrated with copies of the cuts in the English edition, so that it would seem as if the use of the original cuts had not been granted him. We also find Claes **de** Grave copying a cut of J. van Doesborgh's in the year 1517, but he also, according to Mr. W. M. Conway (*Woodcutters of the Netherlands,* p. 314) used single cuts of the Chronicle set in 1517 and 1527, the latter of these dates being an error for 1520 (June 27). No. 29 of Mr. Conway's list, for instance, is found on the title of the 1520 book, the *Somme ruyrael* of J. Boutillier. In 1531, according to the same authority, some cuts of the same Chronicle set appear in **a** book printed by Vorsterman; and some small ornaments used **in** Vorsterman's Dutch *Virgilius* are found in the *Cronike van Brabant* printed by J. van Doesborgh in 1530. This same Chronicle **was** printed for Michiel Hillen, J. van Doesborgh's neighbour, and at least one, probably more than one, of the cuts therein used belonged to Hillen in 1520.

In no sense can J. van Doesborgh be called a printer careful in **the** selection or use of his materials. He borrowed right and left, **of** his neighbours in Antwerp, of France, and probably of Germany: indeed it is in very few cases possible to say positively of any cuts used by him that they were made for the actual position they occupy. It is very probable that the majority of those in the books numbered in Part II. Nos. 2, 3, 4, 18, and 26 to 28, were so made, but in most other cases it is certain that the contrary is the truth. Our printer was quite content to illustrate a mention of a ship in the text with a cut of Jonah and the whale, or to use in the *Dieren Palleys* the same illustration, sometimes sideways or upside down for variety, for several different animals. In this point, however, it must be confessed that he differs little from his contemporaries.

7

It next falls to speak of J. van Doesborgh's connection with Laurence Andrewe of Calais, who was in and after 1527 a printer and bookseller at London. It is established by two books, the first of which is that entitled *The wonderful shape and nature of man*, a compilation translated at Antwerp by Andrewe to be printed by 'Johnes doesborowe booke printer' and 'never in no maternall langage prentyd tyl now.' There is no date to this book, but it is (in spite of the statement just quoted) later than the Dutch original (the *Dieren palleys*), which was printed in 1520. The second book is the *Valuation of gold and silver*, 'printed in the city of Antwerp for Laurence Andrewe,' cited by Herbert [*Typographical Antiquities*, p. 412], who, followed by Berjeau [*Bibliophile illustré*, No. 1 (Aug., 1861), p. 5], held that Andrewe was an apprentice of J. van Doesborgh. There is nothing to confirm this conjecture in the books printed at a later time by Andrewe himself, which show no trace of J. van Doesborgh's influence, but on the contrary resemble closely the productions of English printers of that period, such as Peter Treveris or John Rastell. The wording in the *Wonderful Shape* does not in any way imply the dependence of Andrewe.

This book was translated by Andrewe; but who was responsible for the other English books of this press? We know from Wyer's edition of *The four tokens* that J. van Doesborgh was himself the translator; it was 'translated out of Duche into Englysshe by John Dousbrugh.' In the edition printed by J. van Doesborgh himself the *Four tokens* precede the *Fifteen tokens*, which tract is stated in the book to be translated from the French. It is in fact taken from the second part of *L'art de bien mourir*. Probably the English version is not taken directly from the French, but is a translation of the Dutch text printed in the *Oorspronck* of 1517. The translation does little credit to our printer, if indeed the whole book is to be assigned to him: he displays a woful ignorance of English, inserting purely Dutch words in a haphazard fashion. This is also true of the *New Lands*, as was pointed out by Prof. Arber, but it is not generally true of the English books.

8

Douce, in a manuscript note prefixed to his copy of the *Parson of Kalenborowe*, asserts very positively that in all probability Richard Arnold was the translator of most of them; but he does not say on what evidence he grounds the assertion; it may be a mere conjecture.

The last **book** printed **by** J. van Doesborgh with **a date is** the *Cronike van Brabant* of June 1530, to be sold by M. **Hillen**. After this no certain information concerning him is available, though the name of "Jan van Doesborch" occurs as a printer or bookseller **at** Utrecht about the year 1540 [Ledeboer, *Lijst der boekdrukkers . . . in Noord-Nederland*, Utrecht, 1876; p. 46], and this may possibly shew that he removed to Utrecht at some period after 1530.

It will be seen from the foregoing that we know **very** little of our printer's life between the bounding dates of 1508 **and 1530** or 1540, and nothing outside those dates. No doubt **much more** will eventually be learned respecting him and his contemporaries, many of whom are to an equal or even to a greater degree mere names to us at present.

The types used by Jan van Doesborgh are only two in number. The first type, which he employed almost exclusively, is that which with little variation **was** used by Jacobus de Breda, Henrik de Lettersnider, R. van **den** Dorpe, and Henrik Eckert in the fifteenth, and by almost every printer in the Netherlands in the sixteenth century. The second type, a smaller one, is used only as supplementary **to** the other, and only in two books, the undated *Os facies mentum* and the Oorspronck of 1517. The large letters sometimes found on the title-pages are without exception cut on wooden blocks. This was a common practice with Eckert, Vorsterman, and other printers of that period in **the Low** Countries.

In the printer's marks or **devices** found in J. van Doesborgh's books there are five stages, which follow an obvious order of sequence.

Device 1, which is found only in the *Fifteen tokens,* **consists of** the cut used by R. van den Dorpe as his mark. **In its original** state (as figured in Holtrop's *Monuments*, pl. 111 [72]) **this cut** represents the knight Roland facing the right and winding his horn. From branches which arch overhead hang two shields, one on either side : that on the left bears the arms of Antwerp, that on the right bears an axe, the printer's own cognisance. Below a label gives his name as "Van den dorpe." Before being used by J. van Doesborgh the cut was altered ; the name was erased from the label, and the axe from the right hand shield, not so completely, however, but that a vestige of both handle and blade is discernible.

Device 2, which is, like Device 1, only known to have been used by J. van Doesborgh in a single book, the *Van Pape Jans landendes*, first appears in the *Spieghel der volcomenheit* printed by R. van den Dorpe's widow in 1501 ; it is reproduced by Van der Meersch [*Recherches, etc.*, p. 130]. It differs from Device 1 in being smaller and less artistic ; the label, which is blank, is in the upper part of the field, and the shields, which have changed sides, rest on the ground. The axe was cut out of the left hand shield before the device was used by J van Doesborgh.

Not long, as it would seem, after employing Device 2, our printer adopted a motto of his own, which appears after the colophon of *Van der nieuwer werelt* as "e celo descendit ƒbum quod gnothochyauton," a curiously incorrect quotation from Juvenal xi. 27. It is possible that this use of a motto was only a stop-gap used while Device 3 was being cut.

Device 3 is a very remarkable one. It appears in its complete state [3ᴬ] in two books only, the *Reyse van Lissebone* and the *Langer Accidence*. In a chamber with tiled floor sits a woman on a throne with two steps and a canopy. Over her head is her name 'Auontuere;' in her right hand she holds a sceptre, in her left hand the wheel of fortune. The left side of her face is masked, and a bandage covers her eyes. On her right a man labelled 'gheluck' stands blowing a long hornlike instrument. On her left a similar man called 'ongeluc' blows a smaller instrument of the same kind. Below is an inscription, which reads ΥΝΟΘΟΩΙΑΥΤΟΝ, in which may be recognized the 'gnothochyauton' of the motto in *Van der nieuwer werelt*. The scheme of this device is perhaps derived from a cut used by R. **van den** Dorpe in the book entitled *Van nijeuvont, loosheit, ende practike* [Campbell, *Annales*, No. 1705]. It is thus described by Conway [*Woodcutters*, p. 317]: 'A woman (New Invention) seated between her two lawyers (Practice and Cunning).' In any case the device is an admirable one for a printer in a great commercial city, who printed for a market oversea.

Not long after being cut Device 3 appears to have met with an accident, for with the exception of the two books mentioned above, it is in no case found complete, the side edges in the lower part, **where the** inscription is, being broken away, one side wholly, and the other partially. I call the device in this state 3^{n}. The first dated book in which it is found in this state is the *Oorspronck* of 1517, and it is last used in the *Tdal sonder wederkeeren* of July, 1528. In English books it is usually associated with the arms of England.

It is next necessary to determine the chronological order of the productions of J. van Doesborgh. Only eleven of these have a distinct printed date; accordingly that of the large majority has **to** be ascertained otherwise. Two other books contain indications in the text which enable their position to be fixed with sufficient precision. The thirteen books thus obtained are the following :

Dec., 1508.	Reyse van Lissebone.
(Not after 1516).	Prognostication **for 1516.**
May, 1517.	Oorspronck.
1517.	Causes that be proponed.
(After Jan., 1518).	Letter of B. de Clereville.
1518.	Cronike **van** Brabant.
1518.	Merchant's wife.
5 May, 1520.	Dieren palleys.
8 Nov., 1521.	Van Jason ende Hercules.
12 Dec., 1521.	Die historie van Hercules.
25 June, 1528.	Der IX. Quaesten.
10 July, 1528.	Tdal sonder wederkeeren.
June, 1530.	Cronike van Brabant.

It is noticeable that only four of all these are in English, and that, except the first and the last three, all fall within a period of six years. It will be seen hereafter that, although some of the undated books can be grouped round that dated 1508, and others must be distributed through the two great gaps, yet this period of five years contains a far larger number of books in proportion than any other. It is therefore necessary to assume a great increase of activity at this period from some cause, or an immense destruction of works produced in the other periods of our printer's career. Both may be partly true, but the second cause is probably the more important one.

In endeavouring to fix the dates or chronological sequence of undated books, the main standards of comparison are, speaking generally, two : the types and the illustrations, including devices. In the present case the former fails us ; the type remains the same throughout, and any difference in it which is observable is to be attributed rather to variation in presswork than to any traceable progressive wear of the type. It is therefore necessary to depend on the second standard of comparison, the illustrations : and happily in most cases they are of great help. In the first place, the devices give some aid ; though, except in the relations between 3ᴬ and 3ᴮ, confirmation from other considerations is necessary to determine the order in which they are placed : otherwise there would be no evidence, other than a priori probability, for the precedence in time of the two Van den Dorpe devices. The illustrations, however, shew that the order here assigned to them is the right one. The following is a list of the books which contain devices :

Device 1.	The fifteen Tokens, n.d.
Device 2.	Van pape Jans landendes, n.d.
Motto of Device 3.	Van der neuwer werelt, n.d.
Device 3ᴬ.	Reyse van Lissebone, 1508.
	Long Accidence, n.d.

Device 3[B].　　　　Oorspronck, 1517.
　　　　　　　　　Frederick of Jennen, 1518.
　　　　　　　　　Dieren Palleys, 1520.
　　　　　　　　　Der IX quaesten, 1528.
　　　　　　　　　Tdal sonder wederkeeren, 1528.
　　　　　　　　　Mary of Nemmegen, n.d.
　　　　　　　　　The new lands, n.d.
　　　　　　　　　Virgilius, n.d.

In this list we have before us the three books which in all probability precede the *Reyse* of 1508, the first book with a date.

Turning to the other illustrations, the wood-cut borders used so lavishly by J. van Doesborgh afford valuable assistance, not only by a comparison of their condition in various books, but also by other indications. For instance, the borders in the *Fifteen Tokens* are quite distinct from those found in any other book, except that one or two occur in *Van pape Jans Landendes*. A group of books distinguished by the absence of borders comes next. The book last mentioned belongs to this group, though it still contains a few. With the publication of the *Oorspronck* in 1517 a new period is reached, which lasts to the end of the printer's career. This is marked by a very free use of a large number of borders, none of which are identical with those found in the *Fifteen Tokens*. A reference to the short list prefixed to Part II., and a comparison with the list of borders in Part III., will shew that the books in which no borders are found (Nos. 3, *sqq.*) occupy a position intermediate between the *Fifteen Tokens* and the *Oorspronck*, while the transitional book, No. 2, takes its proper place in the scheme. Thus the order assigned to the earliest books by the device is to some degree confirmed. The evidence afforded by the illustrations proper comes next in order. As this is detailed in Part III., it is only necessary here to state briefly the results obtained.

By the cuts common to both, the *Fifteen Tokens* is shewn to precede the *Oorspronck* of 1517. By the borders it is earlier than

Van pape Jans landendes. The cuts shew that both this last and *Van der nieuwer werelt* precede the *Reyse* of 1508. Thus the *a priori* evidence of the devices is confirmed. The *Long Accidence* is connected with the *Reyse* by the device; the *Short Accidence* has the same initial letter as the *Fifteen Tokens*. The *Os facies mentum* has a cut which is found in the *Fifteen Tokens*; its wood-cut title and its use of Type 2 link it to the *Oorspronck* group.

Turning to this middle group (1516-1521), Borders 18-20 prove *Virgilius* to be earlier than the *Dieren Palleys* of 1520, while the cut common to both shews it to be later than the *Oorspronck*; Borders 18, 21, and one cut make it earlier than *Frederick of Jennen*; but it is impossible to decide whether *Frederick* or *Mary of Nemmegen* is the earlier. Several borders establish the priority of the *Letter of B. de Clereville* [after Jan., 151⅞] to any of these three. The cuts common to the *New Lands* and to the *Dieren Palleys* seem to prove the former to be the later, though Border 20 appears to tell the other way. In this connection Border 23 is also noticeable. The *Wonderful Shape* is undoubtedly later than the *Dieren Palleys*; the *Huys der fortunen* must be placed earlier, as some of its cuts and the type belonging to them are found in the *Dieren Palleys*. The fragment of *Howleglas* belongs to the *Virgilius* group.

In this way the number of books without an approximately determined place in the chronological order has been materially reduced. Of those which remain the places assigned are for the most part conjectural. The *Destructie van Troyen* and some others I have not been able to see: *Euryalus and Lucretia* is not large enough, in the only fragment at present known, to give any clue. *Robin Hood* is placed where it is, because the scarcity of cuts and absence of borders suggest that it belongs to the early period; the date of the tracts with which it is bound (1508) points to the same conclusion. Nothing has yet been said of the *Parson of Kalenborowe*. It is an extremely puzzling book: none of its borders are found elsewhere, and only one of its cuts, which appears in *Frederick of Jennen*. Its general appearance, however, has induced me to place it near the end.

After the rest come three books which are very doubtful. The first may with more or less probability be assigned to J. van Doesborgh. No trustworthy information concerning the other two is forthcoming.

In conclusion, it is necessary to mention the reasons which have led me to exclude the so-called *Arnold's Chronicle*, which is usually attributed to J. van Doesborgh. There can be little doubt that the attribution is an error. In the first place the date is very suspicious. The last events mentioned in the text are the death of Prince Arthur (12 April, 1502) and the election of sheriffs for the year 19 Henry VII. It is not likely, therefore, that it was printed later than 1503; but the *Oorspronck* of 1517 is the earliest dated folio printed by J. van Doesborgh.

Secondly, the style of printing is different from what we know of J. van Doesborgh's method. The identity of the large type proves nothing, as it is universal : the difference of the small type used in the marginalia from that used by J. van Doesborgh is a strong argument. The three-line and larger initials are in no case identical with any found in books by our printer, although the smaller initials seem in some instances to correspond with those in the *Fifteen Tokens*. Leaf-numbering, again, is found in this book, never in any of J. van Doesborgh's productions, and the presence of several eights in the signatures differs from his practice of making up his folio books in fours and sixes only. Marginalia are here used, but never in any book printed by J. van Doesborgh. The small type used for these marginalia resembles that commonly employed by Govaert Back. It is noticeable that an almanack for 1507 in the Bagford Collection is printed with two types apparently identical with those of *Arnold's Chronicle.* This almanack was printed by Adriaen van Berghen, who set up his press in or about the year 1500. An undated edition of Holt's *Lac puerorum*, in the colophon of which his name appears as 'Adriaen van Barrouwe' shews that he also was a printer of English books.

A single leaf of what appears to be an abridged edition of *Arnold's Chronicle* in quarto is among the Bagford fragments. It is signed **c** i, and contains part of the text on fo. lxiiij of the folio edition. This must naturally share the fortunes of the larger edition: there is nothing definite in it to justify any particular ascription.

Many of the points touched on in the preceding pages will receive amplification or commentary in the remarks appended to the collations in Part II., or in the introductory notes prefixed to the list of wood-cuts of the several books in Part III. In all probability a large number of books printed by J. van Doesborgh at present unknown will at some future time come to light ; the constant discovery of fragments of previously unknown books, such as the *Longer Accidence, Howleglas,* or *Euryalus and Lucretia,* shews clearly enough that much yet remains to be done : much were to be hoped from a systematic search made in the libraries, private and public, of the Netherlands ; but it is to be feared that this is at present wholly impracticable.

Part II.
BIBLIOGRAPHY.

D

BIBLIOGRAPHY.

The following abbreviations are used in Part II.:

Hazlitt, HB.   W. C. Hazlitt's *Handbook of early English literature.*
Hazlitt, BC.   W. C. Hazlitt's *Bibliographical Collections and Notes.*
Arber, *Note.*   The Note on Jan van Doesborgh prefixed to Prof. Arber's
    edition of the *Three earliest English books on America.*
Herbert.   Herbert's edition of Ames' *Typographical Antiquities.*

The titles of books less frequently referred to are given in a form
requiring no further explanation.   An asterisk (*) indicates personal exami-
nation of the book or copy to which it is prefixed.

LIST OF BOOKS PRINTED BY JAN VAN DOESBORGH.

1.   The Fifteen Tokens. [Before No. 2.] 4*.
2.   Van Pape Jans landende. [Before No. 3.] 4*.
3.   Van der Nieuwer Werelt. [Before No. 4.] 4*.
4.   Die reyse van Lissebone. Dec. 1508. 4*.
5.   Longer Accidence. [c. 1509?] 4*.
6.   Os, facies, mentum. [c. 1510?] 4*.
7.   Destructie van Troyen. [c. 1510?] F*.
8.   Robin Hood. [c. 1510-15?] 4*.
9.   Euryalus and Lucretia. [c. 1515?] 4*.
10. Shorter Accidence. [c. 1515?] 4*.

---

*1. **The** Fifteen Tokens. n.d. [c. 1505?] 4°.

Collation. A B C⁶ D E⁴, by sheets: 26 ff. 30 ll. Text 150 × 91 mm. Type 1.

Title. HEre beginneth a lytel trea ‖ tyſe the whiche ſpeketh of ‖ the xv. tokens the whiche ‖ ſhullen bee ſhewed afore yᵗ ‖ drefull daye of Jugement. ‖ And who that oure lorde ‖ ſhall aſke rekenyng of eue ‖ ry body of his wordis wor ‖ kis and thoughtes. And who oure lorde wyll ſhe ‖ we vs other xv. tokens . of his paſſion to theym ‖ that been deyeth in dedely ſynne. ‖ [*cut.*]

Fo. 1 b, *cut in borders.* Fo. 2 a: IN this begynnyng ſo ‖ wyl J writte of the xv. ‖ . . .

Fo. 14 b: ❡ Here endeth the xv tokens ‖ [*cut.*]

Fo. 15 a: ❡ And here foloweth who our lord ſhal Jhꞌus x̄p̄s ‖ ſhal come to Jugement.

20

Fo. 17 b, l. 23 : ❡ And here foloweth. who that oure lorde ſhall ‖ ſhewe the blyſſed tokens of his paſſyon . . .

Fo. 22 a, l. 18 : ❡ Here endeth this lytill treatyſe that whiche is ‖ called the xv tokens whiche been late tranſlated ‖ oute of frenſhe into Engliſhe. The whiche been ‖ very neceſſary to euery man and woman to kno ‖ we them. . . .

Fo. 22 b : ❡ And here foloweth the nombre of the ſote ſtap- ‖ pes of oure lorde the whiche hy wente in his paſſi ‖ on and alſo other deuote maters. . . .

End, fo. 26 a, l. 19 : lyff Amen. ‖ [*l. 20 blank*] ‖ ❡ Emprinted by me Johan fro doeſborch dwelli- ‖ ge at Anwerpe by the Jron ballaunce ꝛc. ‖

Fo. 26 b : Device 1.

Copies. *(1) British Museum, C. 25. e. 39 ; wants ff. 13, 14, 18, 23, 24, 25. Measures 186 × 127 mm.

*(2) Oxford : Bodleian Library, bought November, 1891 ; wants leaves 23 and 26. Measures 175 × 123 mm.

References. Hazlitt, HB. p. 609, and BC. III. p. 248 : Arber, "f". A copy sold in the Heber sale (part 5) for £3 : 10.

Remarks. The first part of the present work, comprising the four and the fifteen tokens, is taken from the *Coming of Antichrist* in "L'art de bien mourir." The Four Tokens were separately reprinted by Wyer [British Museum, 4856. a.]. His colophon says that the tract is translated by "John Dousbrugh" from the Dutch. The correctness of this is shewn by the numerous Dutch words that are left in the English version. The Dutch text, no doubt a translation from the French, is found in the *Oorſpronck*, No. 12 below, but the present book shews that it must have existed earlier. The tract called "Signa quindecim" [Hain 14731] is quite different from this. The origin of the latter part (ff. 23 to end) I have not ascertained, but it seems to be, like the rest, a translation from the Dutch, words like "gaet", "menſche" for "go", "man", appearing in it.

*2. Van Pape Jans landendes. n.d. [c. 1506?] 4°.

Collation. A⁴ B⁴, by sheets : 10 ff. : 30 (29-31) ll. Text (30 ll.) measures 150 × 85 mm. Type 1.

Title. ❡ Van die wonderlichedē eñ coſtelicheden ‖ van Pape Jans landendes.· ‖ [*four cuts.*] Fo. 1 b : NV wil ic Pape Jā. ‖ bider graciē gods ‖ . . .

End, fo. 10 a, l. 17 : Amen Ghegeuē in ons heylich pallays ī̄t ‖ Jaer onſer gheboorten v. hōdert eñ ſeuene ‖ [*ll. 19-22 blank*] ‖ ❡ Gheprint Thātwer- ‖ pē. Aen dijferē wage ‖ by my Jan. van ‖ Doeſborch. Fo. 10 b : cut, and device 2.

Copy. *British Museum, C. 32. h. 6 : title slightly damaged. Measures 193 × 129 mm.

References. M. Fred. Muller, *Catalogue of books . . . on America . . .* 1872, 8°, p. 277, No. 2277 : Arber, *Note*, "c".

Remarks. According to M. Muller (*l.c.*) this version differs from all those in other languages, but is least unlike the French. MM. Enschede at Haarlem printed 30 copies with their fifteenth-century types [Muller, No. 2278]. It is quite different from the letter to King Emanuel, which is the usual form in which the story is found, but is substantially the same, though with many additions, omissions, and transpositions, as the text printed at the end of the Romance of the knight Owen, in an edition of about 1478 by G. Le Roy or Barthélemy Buyer at Lyon. The differences between this and the English text (No. 22) suggest an original from which both were translated independently.

3. Van der Nieuwer Werelt. n.d. [c. 1507?] 4°.

   Collation. A B ⁴, 8 ff. 30 and 31 ll. The text in the facsimile measures 149 × 90 mm. Type 1.

   Begin, fo. 1 a: Van der nieuwer werelt oft landtſcap ‖ nieuwelicx gheuödē vädē doorluch ‖ tighē cõn. vā Portugael door dē / ‖ alder beſtē pyloet ofte zeekender d' werelt ‖ [*woodcut.*] ‖ Hoe noyt meeſter oft aſtroninᵹ beſcreuē heeft dat ‖ daer een lädt was bewoët vā mēſchē ofte beeſten. *End,* fo. 8 a l. 20: aerden ſijn. ‖ [*ll.* 21, 22 *blank.*] Gheprent Thantwerpen aen ‖ Dyferen waghe. Bi ‖ Jā vā Doeſborch ‖ [2 *lines blank*] ‖ E celo descendit vbum quod ‖ gnothochyauton ‖ Fo. 8 b, woodcut.

   Copy. The only known copy is now in the Carter-Brown library at Providence, U.S.A. A reprint in facsimile of 25 copies only was issued at Providence in 1874 [*British Museum]. It is also described in M. Frederik Muller's *Catalogue of Books on America*, Amsterdam, 1872, 8°, pp. 5-7, No. 24. A facsimile of the first page is given as a frontispiece to the volume.

   Reference. Arber, *Note,* " b ". Harrisse, *Bibl. Amer. Vetust.*, Additions, No. 15.

   Remarks. It is stated in the book itself that the Dutch version is derived from a Latin translation of the Italian original. This is the letter describing his third voyage written to Lorenzo de' Medici by Vespucci. According to M. Muller, the present version is unique in giving a distinct date for the commencement of the voyage. The motto following the colophon supplies an explanation of the printer's device No. 3.

*4. Die reyse van Lissebone. Dec. 1508. 4°.

   Collation. (a) bC⁴: 12 ff.: moſtly 32 ll. Text (32 ll.) 155 × 100 mm. Type 1.

   Begin, fo. 1 a: Die reyſe vā Liſſebone om te varēna dᴣ eylädt ‖ Naguaria in groot Jndien gheleghen ‖ voor bi Callicuten eñ Gutſchi dair ‖ dye ſtapel is vander ſpecerië ‖ Daer ons wonderlijcke dī ‖ gē wed'uaren zij. eſidair ‖ wy veel gheſië heb ‖ bē / als hier na ‖ gheſcreuē ‖ ſtaet. ‖ Welcke reyſe gheſchiede ‖ door dē wille eñ ghebode des alder ‖ doorluchtichſtē Coñs vā Portegale Emanuel ‖ [*cut.*]

   Fo. 1 b: ALderyrſt quamē wi aent landt vā Canarië dwelck ‖ . . . Fo. 5 a: Die reyſe van Jndien. van Calcoenē. eñ vüdē Nyeuwē ‖ landē de doen geuondē warē gefchyet Jnt iaer ons herē ‖ M vijfhondert in die maent van meerte ‖ Mijn vrient Lauerenti Jck Alberico hebbe in voor ‖ . . .

End, fo. 12 a, l. 12: triangel oft een driecantich hoeck als bouē ghefigureert. Fo. 12 b: Gheprent Thantwerpen . . By my ‖ Jan van Doefborch. Jntiaer ‖ M.D. viij. 1 December ‖ [Device 3 A.]

Copies. 1) *British Museum [C. 32. f. 26], acquired 4 Dec. 1855: measures 191 × 135 mm.

2) In the Carter-Brown library, Providence, U.S.A.

References. The *Athenæum* for 5 Nov. 1892, p. 624, and for 20 Jan. **1894** p. 86, contains letters dealing with the present book and the voyage **which** it describes. In the second letter it is shewn that the date 1500 is an error for 1506. A facsimile reprint of this tract with a translation and introduction by Mr. C. H. Coote, was published (London, B. F. Stevens) in 1894. To this book, which is entitled *The Voyage from Lisbon to India*, 1505-6, readers are referred for all information concerning the subject-matter.

*5. Longer Accidence. n.d. [c. 1509?] 4°.

Collation. A fragment consisting of four leaves, 1, 2, 5 and 6 of sig. **B.** **30 ll.** Text measures 147 × 92 mm. Type 1.

Begin, sig. B i a: peratyf mode of the paffyfe voyce as docere How ‖ . . . **B 2 b,** l. 30: of the prefentens / a participle of the pretertens / 2 ‖ . . . **B 5 a, l.** 1: Semper ftare petūt: nunǭ ftant cōpofitiue ‖ *End*, B 6 a, l. 24: be amauiffe. ‖ [ll. 25, 26 *blank.*] ‖ Hoc prefens opufculū p me Johānē ‖ de Doefborch eft exaratum. ‖ B 6 b: device 3 A.

Copy. *Corpus Christi College, Oxford. This fragment was used to line the boards of a volume printed in 1501. Measures 215 × 153 mm.

Remarks. This is the same Accidence as that printed by W. de Worde " In Caxons hous" at Westminster, about 1496, and subsequently printed by Pynson. The first line in this fragment corresponds to the last line of sig. A 8 2 in Worde's edition. No. 11 is an abridgment of this Accidence.

*6. Os facies mentum. n.d. [c. 1510?] 4°.

Collation. [a⁴.] No signatures: 4 ff.: 21 ll. of each type to a page: types 1, 2.

Title [in large woodcut letters] : Os facies mētū ‖ [cut.] a mouth a face a chyse a toth a throote a tonge roffe of the mouth.

Fo. 1 b: O S facies mentū dens guttur lingua palatū ‖ . . .

End, fo. 4 b, l. 30: Nuncius ac obftetrix et portarius atqʒ ‖ [2 *ll. blank*] ‖ Jmpreffum Antwerpie. per me Jo ‖ hannem de Doefborch. . ·. ‖

Copies. (1) in the Huth collection; *(2) at Britwell (leaves 3, 4 slightly mutilated).

References. Huth Catal. vol. 3, p. 1070; Hazlitt, BC. I. p. 311.

Remarks. A fragment of another Antwerp edition of this little vocabulary, is preserved in the Lambeth Palace library [frag. 17].

7. Die Destructie van Troyen. n.d. [c. 1510-15?] F°.

Collation. a—k. 56 ff. 2 cols. Type 1 ?

Title [l. 1 is probably woodcut]. Die deftructie vā ‖ Troyen die laetfte Ende die fchoone amoreus ‖ heyt van Troylus en der schoonder Breseda ‖ Calcas docht' die een verrader was. ‖ [*Cut.*]

End, fo. 55 b, col. 2. ❡ Hier es voleyndet die hiftorie vā ‖ d'amoreufyt van Troylus eñ Brife ‖ da eñ ooc cortelic ouerlopē die deftruc ‖ tie vā Troyen. Gheprent Thant- ‖ werpen aen dijferen waghe Bi mi ‖ Jan van Doefborch ‖ Fo. 56 blank ?

Copy. The only known copy is (or was in 1869) in the library of the Duc d'Arenberg.

References. The above description is taken from the *Bibliophile Belge* [Bulletin of the Soc. des Bibliophiles Belges], Vol. 4, 1869, p. 18. See also Visser, *Naamlijst* . . . [Amst. 1767, 8°] p. 63 : Meerman, *De l'invention de l'imprimerie* . . . [Par. 1809, 8°] pp. 373-4 : Panzer, I. p. 15, No. 116 : Hain, 5524: Van der Meersch, p. 131.

Remarks. The Bibl. Belge says that this book is probably an imitation of the mystery of the same name of which several editions were printed at Paris and Lyon. Otherwise it would be natural to suppose it a reprint of the earlier edition by R. van den Dorpe; see Campbell, *Annales* . . No. 876.

8. Robin Hood. n.d. [c. 1510-15?] 4°.

Collation. A b⁶ c⁴ d⁶ e⁴, by sheets : 26 ff. : 28-33 ll. : text (33 ll., in facsimile) measures 162 × 88 mm. Type 1.

Begin, fo. 1 a : ❡ Here begynneth a geft ‖ of Robyn Hode. ‖ [*cut.*] ‖ Lythe and liftin gōtilmen yᵗ be of frebore ‖ blode . . .

End, fo. 20 b, last line · There myght no man to thy trufte. ‖ [*i.e. fit* 6, *stanza* 33, *l.* 3.]

Ff. 21-26 unknown.

Copy. Advocates' Library, Edinburgh ; **No. 11 of the volume** containing Chapman and Myllar's early productions. **Wants** ff. 6, 7, 13-18, 21-26.

References. Dickson and Edmond, *Annals of Scottish Printing* . . . [Cambr. (Aberdeen) 1890, 4°] pp. 68 sqq., with a facsimile of leaf 1, and table of types ; it was reprinted in 1827 by Dr. Laing, with the other pieces in the volume.

*9. Aeneas Sylvius: Euryalus and Lucretia. n.d.? [c. 1515?] 4°.

Collation. Fragment of 4 ff., one gathering : 19 ll. left on fo. 2. The text is 88 mm. wide. Type 1.

Fo. 1 a, l. 1 : f Ofias al was this a grete myfdede he defē- ‖ ded . . .

Fo. 2 a, l. 1 : . . . myne frende Eureale and hath late fall of gre ‖ te . . .

Copy. *Signet Library, Edinburgh : a fragment consisting of the upper half of two consecutive leaves from the middle of the piece, with small pieces of two other leaves attached.

Remarks. This fragment, discovered by Mr. E. Gordon Duff in 1891, appears to be an earlier English edition than any previously known. See Hazlitt, HB. p. 588, for three later editions, one of 1560, one of 1567, and **one** imperfect, but of about the same date. This last is a different translation **from** the present text; probably from the Latin. An edition was licensed **to** T Norton in 1569-70 : see Arber's *Transcript of the Registers* . . ., **vol. 1,** p. 189 : Warton's *Hist. of English* **Poetry,** vol. 3, p. **416, note.**

*10. Shorter Accidence. n.d. [c. 1515?] 4°.

Collation. [a⁴.] No signatures. 4 ff.: 31 ll. on fo. 1 a, without headline ; the rest has headline and 29 ll. Text [fo. 3 a] measures 142 × 100 mm. Type 1.

Begin, fo. 1 a :

Accidence

H Ow many partes of reaſo be
there . viij . whyche . viij . now
neſpnowne/ɫbe/adúbe/parti
ciple . . .

End, fo. 4 b, l. 24 : lowyng in one which one in gener only. ¶ [*ll.* 25, **26 blank.**] Emprynted by me Johñ off Doeſborch. ‖

Copy. *Oxford, Bodleian [4° A 18 Art BS.]; perfect : measures 184 × 127 mm.

References. Hazlitt, BC. I. p. 401.

Remarks. This is an abridgment of No. 5. The Bodleian copy is misbound, the title of a copy of Stanbridge's Accidence which follows in the volume being prefixed to it. Hence the description given by Hazlitt is erroneous.

*11. Laet's Prognostication for 1516. [1515-16.] 4°.

Collation. A fragment consisting of the first four **leaves only ; a⁴.** 33 ll. Text measures 163 × 105 mm. Type 1 ?

Begin, fo. 1 a : ¶ The pronoſticaciõ of maiſter **Jaſpar late** of borchloon/ ‖ doctour in aſtrologie of the yere. M.CCCCC.xvi. tranſ ‖ lated into yngliſſh to the honorre of te mooſt noble ꞇ vic- ‖ torious **kynge** Henry the . viij . by your mooſt húble ſub- ‖ iect Nicholas longwater goeuerner of our lady cõception ‖ in ẙ renowmed towne of Andwarp in ſinte Jorge perys ‖ [*l.* 7 *blank.*] ‖ ¶ Prinſipaly takyng for my fundament after folowyng ‖ . . . *End,* **fo.** 4 b, l. 33 : nyng ſo ſhall this yere not be fre of peſtilenſe with apof- ‖

Copies. 1) *British Museum [Harl. MS. (Bagford fragments) 5937. 58]; **fo. 1** only. *2) Trinity College Cambridge [VI⁴. 7. 24]; sheet a only ; measures 202 × 134 mm. This is doubtless the copy sold at D. Laing's sale in 1879. It was acquired in 1882.

References. Hazlitt, BC. II. p. 331. Sinker, *Catal. of Eng. Books,* No. 985.

Remarks. I do not feel certain that J. v. D. is the printer of this book. The four leaves now known to exist afford no test by which the question can be decided.

*12. Den oorspronck onser salicheyt. May 1517. F°.

Collation. A B C⁶ D⁴ E⁶ alternate sixes and fours to Y⁶. AA, BB⁴ CC⁶ DD⁴ alternate to JJ, KK⁶ LL, MM⁴ NN⁶ OO⁴ PP⁶ QQ⁴. 190 ff. 2 cols. 40 ll. Text measures 195 × 146 mm. Types 1, 2.

Title [*ll. 1-2 woodcut, on two blocks, l. 1 red, in relief : l. 2 white on black ground*]. Den. oorspronck ‖ Onſer. ſalicheyt ‖ [*six cuts with the names printed sideways*]. fo. 1 b [*two cuts. To right and left of the upper cut is printed, sideways*]: Cum gracia ‖ Et preuilegio ‖ Fo. 2 a : Die Prologhe.' ‖ DJe heylighe propheta Moyſes wāt hi eē ‖ . . . Fo. 188 b, col. 2, l. 31 : AMEN ‖ [ll. 32, 33 *blank*.] ❡ Hier begint de tafel / inhoudēde die ‖ capittelen des tegenwoerdigē boecx. ‖ . . . Fo. 190 a, col. 2, l. 16 : Telos ‖ [6 *lines blank*] ‖ ❡ Geprent Thantwerpen in de ſtat ‖ ‖ Bi Jan van doeſborch/ie ſeg v dat ‖ Jnt iaer alſmen ſceef . xvij . eñ vijſtien ‖ Jnt leſte vā mey / wient v̇wōd't (hōd't ‖ Js hier miſſet / miſtelt wilttet v̇geuen ‖ Op dꝛ wi mogen comē int ewich leuē ‖ Fo. 190 b: device 3 в within borders.

Copies. *1) British Museum [C. 37. f. 10] ; perfect. Measures 253 × 191 mm. 2) Royal Library, The Hague.

References. Arber, *Note*, "j". Holtrop, *Monuments Typographiques*, p. 5. Le Long, *Boek-Zaal der Nederduytsche Bybels* (Amst. 1732), p. 487 sqq.

Remarks. This is a curious collection of theological treatises, consisting chiefly of a life of Christ, descriptions of the virtues and vices, the last judgment, etc. It contains the Dutch text of the Fifteen Tokens (No. 1) ; but the English version there printed must be several years earlier than the date of this book.

13. Causes that be proponed and tracted . . . [After 12 Nov. 1517.] 4°.

Causes that be proponed and tracted in a Confultacyon of a Journey to be made with the Tokyn of the holy Croffe/ agaynft the Jnfideles and Turkes, and fent to all cryften princes, to thentente that they throughe their good counfell, and wyfe examinacyon, fholde examyne, yf any thynge therin be, that out ought to be encreafed, or mynyffhed ; or yf ought to be correctyd. This done the xij daye of Nouember.

Black letter, with cuts.

Copy. West catalogue, lot 1851, No. 6 ; without printer's name, but apparently by J. van D.

References. Herbert, p. 1533. See also No. 16 below.

Remarks. The Latin original of this tract was printed about the same time
by Michael Hillenius (Hoochstratanus) with the following title, under a
woodcut of the Papal arms: ❡ Propoſita ꝯ tractata in con- ‖ ſultatione Sctē
expeditiöis q̄ ‖ ad Prīcipes mittēda viſa ſunt ‖ (*etc.*) This edition consists of
four leaves in quarto, 44 lines to a page. (Corpus Christi College, Oxford ;
Th. o. 32 [52].) Vanderhaeghen, *Bibl. Belg.,* Ser. 1, P 14.

14. Letter of B. de Clereville. [After Jan. 1518̊.] 4°.

Collation. [a⁴], no signatures. 4 ff. 30 ll. Text measures 149 × 113 mm.
Type 1.

Title. ❡ The Copye of the letter folowynge whiche ſpeci ‖ fyeth of ẏ greateſt
and meruelous viſyoned ‖ batayle that euer was ſene or herde of ‖ And alſo
of the letter ẏ was ſent fro ‖ me the great Turke vnto our ‖ holy fad' ẏ pope
of Rome. ‖ [*cut.*] Fo. 1 b: a cut, followed by a similar title. Fo. 2 a :
Bartholomeus de clere ville to his beloued frende ‖ ẏ lorde of veronoys
hūfray bon messagier. Salute ‖ Fo. 3 a, l. 27 : Wryten in ẏ caſtell of
ville clere / in ẏ yere of our lor ‖ de. M.CCCCC.xvij. in ẏ monthe of
Januarij. *End,* fo. 4 a, l. 21 : . . . Wrytten in our grete ‖ cite of Chayne/
in ẏ yere. vi. M. and of our reigne ‖ the. x. yere ‖ [*l. 24 blank*] ‖ Emprented
in ẏ famous cite of Andwarpe ‖ Be me / Johñ of Dousborowe ‖ Fo. 4 b
blank.

Copies. 1) *Bodleian [Douce C. 247]; perfect : measures 169 × 119 mm.
2) *Britwell. Imperfect, wanting leaf 4 and part of leaf 2. The provenance
of this copy is not known. Measures 167 × 128 mm.
3) Another imperfect copy was sold in Evans' sale of 5 June 1823 (No. 535)
to Thorpe for a guinea.

References. Herbert, p. 1531 : Hazlitt, HB. p. 112 : West Catalogue, lot **1851**
[see Note to No. 16].

15. Chronike van Brabant. 1518. Fo.

Collation. Unknown.
Copy. Royal Library, The Hague.
References. Arber, *Note,* " k " : Conway, *Woodcutters,* p. 314.
Remarks. The edition of 1512, which contains the same cuts, is shewn by the
letters h A e, which are found inside the first initial on the title, to have
been printed by H. Eckert. In it are used some of G. Leeu's woodcut
initials. There is a copy in the British Museum (9405 f.).

16. The lyfe of Virgilius. n.d. [1518?] 4°.

Collation. A B⁴ C⁴ D⁴ E F⁴, signed by sheets. 30 ff. 28, 29 ll., without head-
lines. Text (on fo. 10) 144 × 87 mm. Type 1.
Title [*the first word in large woodcut letters*]: Virgilius. ‖ ❡ THis boke treath of

the lyfe of Virgilius ‖ and of his deth and many maruayles that ‖ he dyd in his lyfe tyme by whychcraft and ‖ nygramanſy thorowgh the helpe of the de ‖ uyls of hell. ‖ [*cut.*] Fo. 1 b blank ; fo. 2 a : ❡ The prologe. ‖ [*l. 2 blank.*] ‖ THis is reſonable to wryght the meruelus ‖ . . . Fo. 2 b : ❡ Howe Romulus cam wich in the fayer tow ‖ ne of Reynes . . . [*etc.*, 3 *lines. The rest of the page is occupied by a cut.*] Fo. 3 a : AS Romulus harde ſay of his broder Re: ‖ *End*, fo. 29 b, l. 9 : the boke of euer laſting blyſſe. Amen. ‖ [*ll.* 10-14 *blank.*] ‖ ❡ Thus endethe the Lyfe of Virgilius ‖ with many dyuers conſaytes that ‖ he dyd Emprynted in the Cy ‖ tie of Anwarpe By me ‖ Johñ Doeſborcke ‖ dwellynge at yᵉ ‖ the camer ‖ porte. ‖ Fo. 30 a The arms of England crowned. Fo. 30 b : device **3 B**.

Copies. (1) *At Britwell, perfeꝗt; measures 169 × 118 mm. * (2) Bodleian [Douce 40], wanting the firſt leaf. Measures 181 × 130 mm.

References. Van der Meersch, pp. 131, 132 : Hazlitt HB. p. 634 : Bradshaw, *Half Century of Notes* . . . No. 49 [see below] : Arber, *Note*, "h ".

Remarks. This is probably a translation of the Dutch version printed about the same date by Vorsterman, which contains copies of some of the cuts in this edition. There is a copy of the Dutch edition in the British Muſeum [1073. b. 32]. The Dutch text is probably a translation from the French, in which language there are two undated editions, one printed by Guillaume Nyuerd, and the other for Jehan Saint Denis. The British Museum has a later edition of the English version, perhaps by W. Copland, about 1550. Bradshaw [*l.c.*] identifies with this edition the " virgilius in englis van 4 quaterni", a copy of which was sold by J. Dorne ; but the faꝗt that the present volume consists of six quires seems to render this impossible. Reprints of this edition were issued (1) by E. V. Utterson in 1812, for private circulation; (2) by W. J. Thoms, *Early English Prose Romances*, vol. 2, in 1828 and 1858. (3) by Prof. H. Morley in the *Carisbrooke Library* in 1889.

Note. In the sale catalogue of the library of James West, P.R.S., 1773, No. 1851, is a volume containing Nos. 13, 14, 16, 17, 18, and 22, together with one book printed by W. de Worde, one by Pynson, and four by Notary. This lot was sold to Ratcliffe for £2 : 17 : 6. In the Ratcliffe sale, however, (1776) only three of the Notary books are to be found in the catalogue. The volume appears in faꝗt to have been split up. No. 13 disappears altogether ; No. 14 found its way at a later time into the Douce colleꝗtion : No. 22 became the property of Thomas Caldecott (1744-1833). At his sale in 1833 it was bought by Thorpe for Grenville (lot 1413) for £25 : 10 : 0. See also Quaritch's *Dictionary of Book Colleꝗtors*, part 4. Nos. 16-18 came into the posseſſion of the duke of Roxburghe, by whom they were uniformly bound in calf, with the ducal arms. In the Roxburghe sale (1812), No. 17 (lot 6377) was sold for £65 : 2 : 0 ; No. 18 (lot 6378) for £67 ; No. 16 (lot 6376) for £54 : 12 : 0, probably to the duke of Marlborough, since in the sale of the White Knights library (7 June 1819) they reappear. No. 17 (lot 1726) was sold to Knell for £44 : 12 : 6 ; No. 18 (lot 2724) to Long-

man for £42; No. 16 (lot 4595) to Triphook for £29 : 8 : 0. No. 17 is
found next as lot 656 in a miscellaneous sale by Evans on 5 June 1823, when
it was sold to Thorpe (for Heber) for £24 : 10 : 0. No. 18 was sold in the
Inglis sale (9 June 1826) to Thorpe for £24. Next comes the Hibbert sale
of 16 March 1829, when Nos. 16 and 18 were sold both to Thorpe for
Heber: No. 18 (lot 5369) fetched £14 : 3 : 6; No. 16 (lot 8400) fetched
£29 : 18 : 6. Lastly all three reappear in part IX. of the Heber sale catalogues
(11 Apr. 1836), when they were sold again to Thorpe for Mr. Christie
Miller: No. 17 (lot 1267) for £16 ; No. 18 (lot 1949) for £16 ; No. 16
(lot 3145) for £25 : 10 : 0.

*17. Frederick of Jennen.   1518.   4°.

Collation. AB⁶ CD⁴ E⁸, signed by sheets. 26 ff. 28, 29 ll. Text measures
(28 ll.) 139 × 86 mm. Type 1.

Title. ❡ This mater treateth of a merchaū ‖ tes wyfe that afterwarde went lyke ‖
a mā and becam a great Lorde and ‖ was called Frederyke of Jennen af- ‖ ter-
warde. ‖ [*cut.*] Fo. 1 b, a cut. Fo. 2 a, l. 1 (ornaments.) ‖ (*l. 2 blank.*) ‖
❡ The prologe. ‖ [*l. 4 blank.*] ‖ (ornaments.) ‖ [*l. 6 blank.*] ‖ Ovre lorde god
sayeth in the gospell / what ‖ . . . Fo. 2 b, below a cut and line of ornaments : ❡ Howe .iiij. Merchauntes met all togyther ‖ in on way whyche
were of iiij. dyuerse landes ‖ and how they wolde all to Parys. ‖ Fo. 3 a : In
the yere of our Lorde god. M.CCCC. ‖ xxiiij. . . .

End, fo. 24 a, l. 6: brynge both you and me. ‖ [2 *lines blank.*] ‖ (ornaments.) ‖
[2 *lines blank.*] ‖ ❡ Thus endeth this lyttell storye of lorde frede- ‖ ryke
Imprȳted ī Anwarpe by me Iohū ‖ Dusborowghe dwellynge besyde ẏ ‖ Camer
porte in the yere of our lor ‖ de god a .M.CCCCC. and ‖ xviij. ‖ [1 *line
blank.*] ‖ (ornaments.) Fo. 24 b, device 3 a. 25 a, cut. 25 b, device repeated.
26 (blank ?) wanting.

Copies. *1) At Britwell: perfect, except for fo. 26, but injured somewhat
by damp. Measures 169 × 118 mm. For its history see note to No. 16.
*2) part of fo. 12, in the British Museum, a Bagford fragment [Harl. 5963,
No. 302, fo. 103].

References. Van der Meersch, p. 132: Hazlitt, HB. p. 212: Herbert,
p. 1533.

Remarks. This is probably a translation from the Dutch, and bears marks of
being by the same hand as Nos. 15, 16, 18, 19 ; the translator was possibly
Lawrence Andrewe, certainly an Englishman : there is no trace of ignorance
of English as in Nos. 1, 22. The original text of this tale appears to be the
" Liebliche Historie von vier Kaufleuten," of which four editions printed in
the fifteenth century are known. 1) An edition *sine nota* [Hain 8750 ;
Muther, *Die deutsche Bücher-Illustration,* 1884, no. 810], of which there is
a copy in the Berlin University Library ; 2) Leipzig, Greg. Bötticher, 1495
[Muther 693], of which there are copies at Hannover [Bodemann, *Incunabeln*

29

der *k. Bibl. zu H.*, no. 156], and in the Berlin University Library. 3) Nürnberg, Hans Mair, 1498 [Hain 8751, Muther 440]. 4) Nürnberg, Hans Mair, 1499 [Hain 8752, Muther 441]. No edition of the Dutch version is known from which the present text can have been translated; but a copy of a later edition, printed by Vorsterman at Antwerp on 8 Feb. 1531, is in the Ghent University Library. It is entitled: "vā. heer. frederick vā Jenuen in Lombardië een warachtige historie . . ." See Vanderhaeghen, *Bibliotheca Belgica*, Ser. 1, F 5. Two leaves of another English edition in quarto, with 32 lines to a page, perhaps printed by W. de Worde, are among the Douce fragments in the Bodleian. These leaves, with a facsimile of the woodcut, were reproduced by **Dr.** Furnivall in 1871 at p. xxvi of "**Captain Cox** and his books," published by the Ballad Society; and again in 1887 for the New Shakspere Society [ser. vi., No. 14; pp. 26-28 (R. Laneham's Letter)]. In the British Museum [C. 20. c. 42 (6)] is a later edition, **printed** by Abr. Vele, which is a close reprint of the present edition.

⁕18. Mary of Nemmegen. [1518-19?] 4°.

Collation. A B⁶ C D⁴. 20 ff. 28 ll. Text measures 138 × 85 mm. Type 1.

Title. ❡ Here begynneth a lyttell ſtory that was of a ‖ trwethe done in the lande of Gelders of a may ‖ de that was named Mary of Nēmegen ẙ was ‖ the dyuels paramoure by the ſpace of .vij. yere ‖ longe. ‖ [*cut.*] Fo. 1 b, below a cut: Iɴ the tyme when Duke Arent was taken ‖ . . . Fo. 19 a, l. 19: brynge bothe you and me amen. ‖ [*2 lines blank.*] ‖ (ornaments.) ‖ [*1 line blank.*] ‖ ❡ The concluſyon. ‖ [*ll. 26-28 blank.*] Fo. 19 b, l. 1: ❡ Al this in this boke conteyned is for a trewth ‖ and if that ye wyll nat beleue me that was the ‖ fyrſt maker of this boke . l. 12: to the whyche blyſſe brynge both you and me. ‖ AMEN. ‖ [1 *line blank.*] ‖ (ornaments.) ‖ [1 *line blank.*] ‖ ❡ Thus endeth this lyttell treatyſe Jmprynted ‖ at Anwarpe by me Johñ Duiſbrowghe dwel- ‖ lynge beſyde the camer porte. ‖ Fo. 20 a: cut. 20 b: Device 3 B.

Copy. *At Britwell, the only copy known; measures 169 × 118 mm. For its history see Note to No. 16.

References. Herbert, p. **1532**: Hazlitt, **HB**. p. **381**: Arber, *Note*, "i": Van der Meersch, p. **131.**

Remarks. This tract is doubtless translated from the Dutch, but no edition of the Dutch text printed in the sixteenth century is known. There are however two editions of the seventeenth century. The first of these, which probably represents more or less faithfully the original text from which the English version is derived, was printed by Pauwels Stroobant at Antwerp in in 1615. A copy of this edition, which has several woodcuts, is in the University Library at Ghent. It has been twice reprinted, once in 1853 by the Maetschappy der Vlaemsche Bibliophilen of Ghent, the editor being Baron J. de Saint-Genois, and again by Prof. J. van Vloten at The Hague in 1854. The other edition of the Dutch text was printed at Utrecht in 1608 by Herman van Borculo. It has not been reprinted, but its variant readings, and other information concerning it, are given by Prof. van Vloten's edition. It differs from the Antwerp edition in having been expurgated by a Protestant editor, who omitted passages of a Catholic tendency. There is a copy of this edition in the Royal Library at the Hague.

*19. Tyll Howleglas. n.d. [c. 1519?] 4°.

    Collation. A fragment. J⁴ K⁶. Wanting part of J 1, and K 3-4. 28 ll. Text measures 138 × 85 mm. Type 1.

        Sig. J 1 a, l. 1 : with a good wyll and than toke Howleglas ỹ ‖ . . [" *How Howleglas serued a shoemaker*"] J 1 b, l. 14 : ❡ Howe Howleglas **folde** tourdes for fat. J 2 b, l. 17 : ❡ Howe Howleglas serued a Tayler. J 4 a, below a cut : ❡ Howe Howleglas defeyued a wynedrawer ‖ in Lubeke. K 2 a, l. 25 : ❡ Howe Howleglas becam a maker of fpecta- ‖ kles . . . K 5 b, l. 28 : ❡ Howe Howleglas was byd for a gefte. End, K 6 b, l. 27 : his Hoofte and the hooftayfe.

    Copy. * British Museum [C. 34. f. 51], rescued from a binding : presented in 1887. Ff. 1-3 are bound after ff. 4-8. Measures 193 × 152 mm.

    Remarks. Two editions printed by R. Copland [British Museum, C. 21. c. 53 and 57] are as regards the text almost word for word the same as this edition, even the spelling being for the most part preserved ; but the chapter headings sometimes differ. A third edition printed by one of the Coplands is also known. See Dr. Furnivall's *Captain Cox and his books* [Ballad Society, Lond. 1871], p. xlviii. A good account of Eulenspiegel, especially of this English version (as printed by Copland), is given by C. H. Herford, *The literary relations of England and Germany* [Camb. 1886], p. 283 *sqq.* J.M. Lappenberg, *Dr. Thomas Murner's Ulenspiegel* [Leipz. 1854], p. 153, describes an edition in Dutch, printed at Antwerp by M. Hillen, without date. This Dutch text contains only a selection of the tales found in the German original ; the fact that the English version is identical in this respect seems to shew clearly that it is a translation from the same Dutch text, though not necessarily from this edition of it.

20. Thuys der fortunen. n.d. ? [before 1520?] F°?

    Thuys der fortunen ende dat huys der doot.

    Fr. Olthoff : *De Boekdrukkers boekverkoopers en uitgevers in Antwerpen*, 1891, p. 26, mentions a copy as having been sold at Antwerp in the De la Faille sale, 1878, for 135 fr.

*21. Der Dieren Palleys. 5 May 1520. F°.

    Collation. A B⁶ C-V⁴ X⁴ Y⁴ A 2-H h⁴. 124 ff. 2 cols. usually 38, 39 ll. Text (38 ll.) measures 188 × 145 mm. Type 1.

Title. [*A large woodcut with figures of animals, birds and fishes: at top a band with three half-length portraits named above, in type:*] Plinius Albertus magnus Dyaſcorides. [*In the centre of the page is a square space containing the title: ll. 1-2 are printed from three blocks placed rather sideways; l. 1 is white on red, l. 2 red on white.*] D e r d i e r ē ‖ p a l l e y s : eñ ‖ Die ʋgaderinge vandē beeſten d' ‖ Aerdē. Vandē vogelē d'lucht. Vā- ‖ dē viſſchen eñ monſtrē d' waterē. ‖ Fo. 1 b, below a cut : Cum Priuilegio et Gracia ‖ Fo. 2 a : Die proleghe ‖ *End,* fo. 123 a, col. 2, l. 12 [*ll. 10, 11 blank*] : Hier is volbracht dat derde tractaet ‖ des boecs vandē viſſchen / god heb lof. ‖ daermen in mercken mach die macht ‖ eŋ grote wond'lijcheyt ſijnd' wercken ‖ [*l. 16 blank*] ‖ Gheprent bi my Jan van doeſborch ‖ Thantwerpen. Jnt iaer ons heeren ‖ M.CCCC. ende .xx. den vijſten ‖ dach in Meye. ‖ [*cuts.*] Fo. 123 b, 124 a blank. Fo. 124 b : device 3 в in borders.

Copies. *1) British Museum (458. d. 1); perfect. Measures 261 × 178 mm. *2) British Museum (1256. h. 3); perfect, but very short. Measures 242 × 181 mm.

References. Panzer, IX. 344. 42ᵇ : Arber, *Note,* "1".

Remarks. No. 23 is a translation of this book, which appears to be based on the old 'Liber Bestiarum.'

*22. Of the New Lands. n.d. [c. 1520?] 4°.

Collation. A⁶ B C⁴ D⁶ E⁴. 24 ff. 29 and 30 ll. Text (30 ll.) measures 148 × 84 mm.

Title [*enclosed in borders*]. ❡ Of the newe lādes and of ẏ people ‖ found by the meſſengers of the kyn ‖ ge of portẏgale named Emanuel. ‖ [*l. 4 blank.*] ‖ Of the .x. dyuers nacyons cryſtened. ‖ [*l. 6 blank.*] ‖ Of pope Johñ and his landes / and of ‖ the coſtely keyes and wonders molō ‖ dyes that in that lande is. ‖ [*cut.*] Fo. 1 b : four woodcuts. Fo. 2 a, ll. 1, 2 blank. l. 3 : Hᴇʀᴇ a ‖ forety ‖ mes in the ‖ yere of our ‖ Lorde god. ‖ M.CCC. ‖ C.xcvi. τ ſo ‖ . [*fo. 14 b is blank.*] *End,* fo. 24 a, l. 11 : dred . and ſeuen ‖ [*l. 12 blank.*] Emprenteth by me Johñ of Doeſborowe ‖ [*cut.*] Fo. 24 b : device 3 в.

Copies. *1) British Museum [G. 7106]; perfect ; measures 179 × 119 mm. *2) A fragment among the Douce fragments in the Bodleian, consisting of leaves 17 and 22.

References. Arber, "The first three English Books on America," a reprint : West Catalogue (see No. 16), lot 1851, No. 5 ; Herbert, p. 1533 ; Hazlitt, HB. p. 478 ; Bibl. Grenvilliana, I. p. 24. Harrisse, *Bibl. Amer. Vetust.,* No. 116 ; Coote, *The Voyage from Lisbon to India,* note 29.

Remarks. This book is made up of several parts. Fo. 2, describing a voyage of 1496 (the only part in this volume relating to America), appears to be translated from a lost book, to which the cut on fo. 2 a, and one in the *Dieren Palleys,* may have belonged. Ff. 2-7 a are a free translation from ff. 1 b- 6 b of the *Reyse van Lissebone.* The paragraph on fo. 7 b is an expansion of a line and a half on fo. 1 b of the *Reyse*, which are omitted in the translation. Fo. 8 a is taken from fo. 12 a of the *Reyse*; but the two last lines are interpolated. The second part of the book is a translation of a Dutch version of the *Tractatus de decem nationibus christianorum*, which is usually appended to the *Itinerarius* of Johannes de Hese. The third part is the same tract as No. 2 (*Van Pape Jans landende*), but appears to be an independent translation from a Latin or French original; see remarks on No. 2 above. A curious point is the insertion of the name of the king of England near the end; this is not found in the Dutch **text**.

*23. The Wonderful shape. n.d. [after 1520.] F°.

   Collation. a⁶ b—k, L, m—u⁴. 82 ff. 2 cols. 40, 41, 42 ll. Text (40 **ll.**) measures 197 × 146 mm. Type 1.

   Title [*unknown.*] Fo. 2 a, col. 1, l. 1 : ❡ Prologus. ‖ [*l. 2 blank.*] ‖ J N the ‖ name ‖ of ower ‖ fauiour ‖ crifte Je ‖ fu ma- ‖ ker ꝛ re ‖ demour ‖ of al mā ‖ kynd / J ‖ Laurēs ‖ ãdrewe ‖ of ỹ tow ‖ ne of Ca ‖ lis haue ‖ tranfla ‖ ted for ‖ Johñes ‖ doefbo- ‖ rowe booke prenter in the cite of And ‖ warp this pfent volume deuided in ‖ thre parts which was neuer before ꝯ in no maternall langage prentyd tyl ‖ now/ . . . Part 1 ends fo. 39 b ; part 2 ends 63 a, col. **1.** *End,* fo. 81 b, col. 1, l. 1, below a cut : Hᴇere endyth the wonder ꝯ fulle fhape ꝛ nature ỹ our ꝯ sauyor cryſt Jhefu hath created in beftys / ferpētys ꝯ on ỹ erth / fowles in ỹ ayre ꝯ and fifthes ꝛ monfters in **the water** ꝛ ꝯ fee / . . . *ib.* l. 18: Amen ꝯ [*l. 19 blank*] ‖ Tranflated be me **Laurens** andrewe ‖ of the towne of Calis / in the famous ꝯ cite of Andwarpe ‖ Emprented be me Johū of ‖ Doefborowe ꝯ [*border.*] *Ib.* col. 2: four cuts with names, five lines of text, and border. Fo. 82, *unknown.*

   Copy. *Cambridge, University Library ; measures 232 × 172 mm. Imperfect, wanting ff. 1, 6, 8, 9, 26, 79, 80, 82. Ff. 52, 78 are torn. It was bought by one John Reynoldes in 1591 [inscription on fo. 39].

   References. Herbert, pp. 1531, 1822 ; he dates it 1511. [Why ?] Hazlitt, HB. p. 8, calls it "The Noble life and natures . . ." ; BC. I. p. 474. Arber, *Note,* "m " : Berjeau, *Bibliophile,* I. p. 5.

24. Van Jason ende Hercules. 8 Nov. 1521. F°.

   Collation. A⁶ B—L⁴. 4 b ff. 2 cols. Type 1 ?

   Title [l. 1 is probably woodcut]. Van Jafon eñ. ‖ Hercules. ‖ ❡ De wonderlike vreemde hiftorien. Hoe dat die edel vrome Jafon ghewan dat gul- ‖ denvlies Eñ vā noch veel wond'like auōtueren die Jafon met die fchone Medea had ‖ de. Eñ voert vandē alder ftereften Hercules / die wond'like feyten vā wapenen in orlo- ‖ ghen dede / doe hi Troyen twee reyfen deftrueerde. Eñ hoe hi vacht tegens vreemde wō- ‖ derlike beeften die hi al verwan. En tis genuechlick eñ wonderlick om te horen lefen ꝯ [*Four cuts.*]

End, fo. 46 a. ¶ Gheprent Tantwerpen bi mi Jan ‖ van Doefborch wonende op die ‖ Lombaerde Vefte. Inden ‖ iare ons heeren .M.‖CCCCC. eñ XXI. ‖ opten achftē ‖ in Nouē ‖ ber. ‖

Copy. The only copy known [in a private library?] is bound with No. 25 and Boccaccio's *Histoire des hommes et femmes celèbres* printed by Claes de Grave in 1525-6.

Reference. *Bibliophile Belge*, Vol. 4, 1869, p. 14 (Analecta-Biblion).

Remarks. According to the *Bibl. Belge* this work has no connection with that of Raoul Le Fèvre. The part relating to Hercules is omitted here, and was printed separately as a sort of second part ; see No. 25.

25. Die historie van Hercules. 12 Dec. 1521. F°.

Collation. a—m⁴. 48 ff. 2 cols. Type 1 ?

Title [*l.* 1 *is probably woodcut*]. Die hiftorie ‖ Van den ftercken Hercules / Die veel wonderlike dinghen in fijn leuen heeft ‖ ghedaen. Syn gheboerte was wonderlic / eñ fijn leuen was auontuerlic / wāt ‖ hi menich v̄uaerlic beefte verflaghen heeft. ghelijc men in die hiftorie hier na ‖ verclaren fal. En fi is feer auontuerlic eñ ghenuechlic om lefen. ‖ [2 *cuts and a border.*]

End, fo. 48. · ¶ Hier eyndet die hiftorie eñ dat leuen vanden vromen Hercules / met die twee ‖ deftructien van Troyen / die door Hercules gefchieden. Eñ iffer ye ‖ mant die de derde deftructie van Troyen begheert te wetē ‖ daer de vrome Hector v̄flaghen was / dats ghe ‖ prent in een and'boeck geheten Die de ‖ ftructie vā Troyen. Eñ dit boeck ‖ is Thantwerpē geprent bi ‖ mi Jan van Doefborch ‖ wonende op de ‖ Lōbaer ‖ de ‖ vefte ‖ in den Aren ‖ van die vier euangeliftē ‖ Jn den iare ons heeren duyfent vijf ‖ hondert en .Xxi. opten twalefften dach van December ‖ [*Cut.*]

Copy. The only known copy is bound with No. 24, q. v.

Reference. *Bibliophile Belge*, Vol. 4, 1869, p. 16.

*26. The Parson of Kalenborowe. n.d. [after 1520?] 4°.

Collation. A⁶ B⁴ C⁶ D⁴ E⁶. 26 ff. 28 ll. Signatures irregular. [Fo. 3 is signed C ij, fo. 4 A iij ; the 3rd leaves of B, C are signed as ij and the fourth leaf of D is signed D ij.] Type 1. ·

Begin. Ff. 1, 2 unknown. Fo. 3 a : come to it and all oncouered ī fuche maner that ‖ . . . *ib.* l. 16 (l. 15 blank): ¶ Howe the parfon be his wyles cau ‖ feth the churche to be couered. ‖

End, fo. 25 b, l. 28 : and after that he changed benefice for another ‖ Fo. 26 unknown.

Copy. *Oxford, Bodleian Library [Douce K. 94]; wanting ff. 1, 2, 26.

References. Herbert, p. 1531 : Hazlitt, HB. p. 314.

Remarks. The German rhymed original, on which the present text is based, by Philip Frankfurter, is reprinted in Hagen's *Narrenbuch*, 1811, where a long note is given, and some prose versions mentioned, all, however, of far later date than the present edition. Gödcke, *Geschichte der deutschen Dichtung* Bd. i, pp. 116, 117, gives copious references, mentioning a *sine nota* edition of the fifteenth century in the Stadtbibliothek at Hamburg. Weller, *Repertorium typographicum*, No. 34, assigns this edition to the first quarter of the sixteenth century. It has 36 woodcuts. This text has been reprinted in Kürschner's *Deutsche National-Litteratur*, vol. 11, pp. 7-86. Two leaves of an early edition of a version in Low German are now in the Royal Library at Berlin. See the *Jahrbuch des Vereins für niederdeutsche Sprachforschung* [1887], Bd. XIII., p. 129 sqq., where the English text is reprinted in full from the Douce copy. The "Pfaff von Kalenberg" was named Wigand von Theben. A description of the Douce copy is given by C. H. Herford, *The Literary Relations of England and Germany*, p. 272 sqq., who also gives an account of the origin of the tale. Douce supposes the translator to be Richard Arnold; but there is no evidence in favour of this view. It is remarkable that with the exception of a single cut, none of the ornaments in this book are found in any other of Doesborgh's productions at present known.

27. **Der IX quaesten.** 25 June 1528. 4°.   •

Collation. A—H⁴. 32 ff. Type 1?

Title [*the first line is woodcut*]. D$_{IX}^{er}$ quaesten ¶ warachtighe historien. **Als vā** Jeroboam Achab / ¶ Joran ioden. Caym Nero Pylato heydē Ju ¶ das Scharioth Machamet Juliano apsto ¶ ta Kerstenen / die alle een onsalich ¶ eyne hadden. ¶

End, fo. 32 b. ❡ Gheprt bi Jā vā Doesborch. Jnt iaer ¶ van .xxviij. den .xxv. dach vā Junio. ¶ ❡ Cum gracia et puilegio. ¶ [Device 3 b.]

Copy. The only known copy passed from the collection of M. van Coetsem to that of M. Capron, at whose sale in 1874 it was bought for the University Library at Ghent for 950 fr.

References. *Bibliophile Belge*, Vol. 4, 1869, p. 60 for the description, and Vol. 9, 1874, p. 332 for its occurrence in the Capron sale of 6 Apr. 1874, where it was lot 478.

Remarks. These curious 'Lives of nine bad men' are described at some length in the *Bibl. Belge*. The author appears to be unknown.

28. **Tdal sonder wederkeeren.** 10 July 1528. 4°.

Collation. **A—D⁴.** 16 ff. Type 1?

Title [l. 1 *is woodcut, printed in red*]. **Tdal** sond' wed'keerē ¶ ❡ Oft Tpas der Doot. ¶ [*Cut.*]

End, fo. 16 b. ❡ Gheprent bi Jan van Doesborch ¶ Jnt Jaer van .xxviij. den .x. ¶ dach van Julius ¶ ❡ Cum gracia et puilegio. ¶ [Border: device 3 b.]

Copy. The only known copy passed through the Lammens, van Coetsem and Capron collections, and is now in the Bibliothèque Royale at Brussels.

References. Vanderhaeghen, *Bibliotheca Belgica*, Ser. 1, C 24. For the Capron sale, in which it was lot 481, see the *Bibliophile Belge*, 1874, p. 332. The piece was reprinted by the Société des Bibliophiles Belges, at the end of the French original, edited by M. Jules Petit [Brussels 1869], with facsimiles of ff. 1 a and 16 b.

Remarks. For a discussion of the authorship of this poem, see M. Petit's preface. It is a translation in nine-line stanzas by Colyn Coellin of Brussels of the French poem by Pierre Michault entitled *Le pas de la mort*. It is remarkable as being the only poetical piece known to exist from the press of J. v. Doesborgh.

*29. Cronike van **Brabant**. June 1530. F°.

Collation. A-K⁴, Aa-Zz⁴, AA-ZZ⁴, a-z⁴, ⨯⁴. 320 ff. 2 cols. 42 ll. **Text** measures 207 × 148 mm. Sig. Cc 3 to Dd 4 are double leaves, **pasted** together and folded. Type 1.

Title [*ll.* 1, 2 *are **woodcut***]. Van . brabant . die . ‖ excellente . Cronike . ‖ Van Vlaenderē / **Hollāt / Zeelant int generael.** Vanden oorfpronck des lants vā Ghelre / **ende ‖ oot die afcomſte** der hertogen van Ghelre. Vā dat ſticht **ende** van die **ſtadt vā Wtrecht** / hoe ſi ‖ comen ſijn onder den keyſer Karolo. Ende van 'de nieuwe geſten gheſchiet bi onſen prince eñ ‖ keyſer Karolo / tottē iare. M.CCCCC. eñ. xxx. in Junio. Ende noch veel ander vreemde geſtē ‖ die in ander Cronijcken niet en ſijn ‖ [*cut*] ‖ ¶ Deſe boecken vintmen te cope **tot** Michiel vā Hoochſtraten in den rape ‖ Fo. 1 b blank. Fo. 2 a : D Je tafele beghint hier ‖   *End,* fo. 320a, col. 2. Fo. 320 b : ¶ Gheprent tot Antwerpen op die Lombaerde ‖ veſte / bi mi Jan van Doeſborch / int iaer ons ‖ heren M. CCCCC. xxx. in Junio. ‖ [*cut.*]

Copies. *1) British Museum [9415. b.]; perfect; measures 273 × 185 mm. **This** copy formerly belonged to the duke of Sussex. 2) Royal Library, The Hague. *3) The title, colophon, and numerous cuts from a cut up copy are in the volume lettered *Douce prints* 173 in the Bodleian Library.

References. **Arber, *Note*,** " k " : ‖ Conway, *Woodcutters of the Netherlands*, p. 314.

DOUBTFUL BOOKS.

*30. **The** valuation of gold and silver. **n.d.** 8°.

Collation. a b c⁸, signed by sheets. 24 ff. 20 lines for the most part. Text (20 ll.) measures 97 × 69 mm. Type 1.

Title. ¶ The valuacyō of golde and fyluer ‖ made i ẏ yere . M.C.CCC. lxxxxix. . ‖ holde i the marke vnce englice quar ‖ t' troye. dewes and aes The maner ‖ for to weight wyth pēnes and gray ‖ nes and herein is ſett ẏ fygures of ẏ ‖ ſpaynyſh and Poortyngalyſh doca ‖ tes whiche is now ‖   ¶ The golde fleys ‖ [*cut*] ‖ The phūs gyldon ‖ [*cut*]. *End,* fo. 24 a, l. 21 : The cruyſſades ij d xviij grayn ‖ fo. 24 b : Two cuts.

Copy. *British Museum [C. 21. **a**. 54]; perfect, but much worn. Measures 125 × 89 mm. On the title page is written, "Wm Herbert. 1786."

References. Herbert, p. 1529, describes this copy; but on the flyleaf he has written a reference to p. 412 of his book, on which mention is made not of this, but of the other edition, No. 32. Hazlitt, BC. III. p. 98.

Remarks. The size of the book, and the character of the cuts on the last page, render the attribution to J. v. D. doubtful. The imposition is extremely faulty, which looks as if the printer was unaccustomed to print books in octavo; the use of a cross stroke through ll is not confined to J. van Doesborgh, though commonly used by him. In the *Bibliophile Belge*, Vol. 14, 1879, p. 380, is given a facsimile of part of a broadsheet relating to the coinage, printed "aen dijseren waghe," in all probability, like Campbell 1733, by R. vanden Dorpe, about 1499-1500. A strong argument in favour of J. van Doesborgh as the printer of the present work is the fact that the two cuts of coins given in the facsimile are from the same blocks, in a much better state, as the cuts found here on ff. 19 b, 20 a (the French blanks).

31. On the Pestilence.

A copy of a treatise on the Pestilence, possibly printed by J. v. D., is said to exist in the library of the late Maurice Johnson, Esq., of Spalding. A search among that part which is still kept at Spalding produced no result.

32. The valuation of gold and silver.   n.d.

The valuacion of Golde and Siluer.   Made in the famous Citie of Antwarpe, and newely Translated into Englifhe by me Laurens Andrewe/
    Emprentyd in the famous Cite of Andwarpe.

Reference. Herbert, p. 412, who makes no mention of any copy as being known to him.

Remarks. There can be little doubt that this book as described is a production of Jan van Doesborgh's press. There seems to have been some confusion in Herbert's mind between this edition and that mentioned on p. 1529, for which see No. 30 above.

PART III.

49

§ 1. THE WOODCUT ILLUSTRATIONS.

The following abbreviations are used in Part 3 for books therein cited. The measurements given are all in millimetres.

1. FT. The Fifteen Tokens.
2. PJ. Van Pape Jans landendes.
3. NW. Van der Nieuwer Werelt.
4. RL. Die Reyse van Lissebone.
12. O. Den Oorspronck.
14. L. Letter of B. de Clereville.
16. V. Virgilius.
17. FJ. Frederick of Jennen.
18. MN. Mary of Nemmegen.
19. H. Howleglas.
21. DP. Der Dieren Palleys.
22. NL. Of the New Lands.
23. WS. The Wonderful Shape.
26. PK. The Parson of Kalenborowe.
29. BC. The Brabant Chronicle of 1530.

1. The Fifteen Tokens.

The woodcuts in this book fall into two main divisions. The first (A), illustrating the tokens, seem to be imitations of those used by A. Vérard's printer in the English edition of the *Ars moriendi* of 1503. The second (B), mostly very small, illustrate the Passion. The origin of these is not known to me.

There are in addition one or two cuts (C) not belonging to either of the above sets, and a large initial, for which see § 3. The cut on fo. 1 b is by the same hand as the figures of female saints in the *Brabant Chronicle*.

The broken state of the enclosing lines of the " A " cuts suggests their having
been used before. A few of them have double lines, like the *Oorspronck* set
A. The following list is incomplete, as neither of the known copies contains
leaf 23.

1. Sig. a 1 a.   Men and women mad.   [A.]   64 × 75.
2. a 1 b.   A doctor writing at his desk.   [C.]   126 × 81.
3. a 4 a.   The sea, with fishes, rising in a cone.   [A.]   66 × 75.
4. a 5 a.   The sea sinks into the earth.   [A.]   66 × 74.
5. a 5 b.   Merman and mermaid raising their arms.   [A.]   63 × 73.
6. a 6 b.   The sea burning with fire.   [A.]   52 × 58.
7. b 1 a.   Trees sweating blood : birds, one with a worm.   [A.]   65 × 74.
8. b 1 b.   Buildings falling to pieces.   [A.]   66 × 73.
9. b 2 b.   Rocks clashing together.   [A.]   65 × 76.
10. b 3 a.   Earthquake : in front, a woman falling; at back, animals.   [A.]
   65 × 75.
11. b 3 b.   Rocks [14] floating in the sea.   [A.]   65 × 74.
   b 4 a.   = No. 1, more broken.
12. b 4 b.   Skeletons lying.   [A.]   64 × 76.
13. b 5 a.   Stars falling; below, animals howling.   [A.]   65 × 75.
14. b 6 b.   All men and women fall dead.   [Cut much injured.   A.]   65 × 75.
15. c 1 b.   Men and women arise from graves on land and in sea.   [A.]   66 × 73.
16. c 2 b.   A man with his hands bound is dropt down a well by two men:
   king behind.   [*Oorspronck* set A : C.]   70 × 70.
17. c 6 a.   The last judgment, with instruments of Passion.   [A.]   89 × 67
18. c 6 b.   Crucifix, T shape.   [B.]   47 × 48.
19. c 6 b.   Instruments of Passion ; a heart in centre.   [B.]   22 × 54.
20. d 1 a.   Pillar and scourge.   [B.]   37 × 14.
21. d 1 b.   Crown of thorns.   [B.]   18 × 16.
22. d 1 b.   Heart pierced by a spear.   [B.]   36 × 13.
23. d 2 a.   Two pierced hands.   [B.]   36 × 18.
24. d 2 a.   Two pierced feet.   [B.]   19 × 13.
25. d 2 a.   Angel holding a cross.   [C.]   58 × 40.
26. d 2 a.   Birch rod and scourge.   [B.]   30 × 17.
27. d 2 b.   Seamless robe.   [B.]   36 × 25.
28. d 2 b.   Head with eyes bound, and halo.   [B.]   31 × 21.
29. d 3 a.   Rope tied in a coil.   [B.]   35 × 11.
30. d 3 b.   Head spitting (placed sideways).   [B.]   19 × 19.
31. d 3 b.   Hand pulling hair or beard.   [B.]   18 × 16.
32. d 3 b.   Three dice.   [B.]   16 × 19.
33. d 3 b.   Money coming out of a bag.   [B.]   17 × 16.
34. d 4 b.   Virgin and Child.   [C.]   42 × 35.
35. d 4 b.   Small kneeling figure.   [A side piece.   C.]   42 × 22.
36. e 2 a.   Christ before Caiaphas.   [Worn : C.]   43 × 55.
37. e 2 b.   Christ scourged by two men.   [C.]   43 × 55.

38. e 2 b.   Christ seated in robe and crown.   Two men with a stick twist the
            crown. [Double lines : C.]   55 × 61.
39. **e** 3 a.   Procession : Christ bearing the cross. [C.]   44 × 73.
40. e 3 b.   Crucifixion.   [Double lines : C.]   99 × 70.
41. e 4 b.   Device No. 1.

2. Van Pape Jans landendes.

Nearly all the cuts used here reappear in the *New Lands* in an inferior condition.
    All except No. 10, and perhaps No. 7, are by the same hand.

  1. Fo. 1 a.   Man with calf's head carrying a large fish on his back.   62 × 27.
  2. 1 a.   Elephant with howdah.   63 × 28.
  3. 1 a.   Griffin flying with a man in his claws.   63 × 28.
  4. 1 a.   Three boys and three ostriches. [A break in the top line not found in
          NL.]   64 × 64.

    2 a.   = No. 2.
  5. 2 b.   Naked savage with one eye carrying club.   62 × 27.
  6. 3 a.   Similar savage with horse's hoofs.   61 × 28.
    4 a.   = No. 4.
  7. 4 b.   Circular cut of Sagittarius with a double line. *diam.* 37.
  8. 5 a.   Phœnix on the fire.   63 × 28.
    5 b.   = No. 3.
    7 a.   = No. 1.
  9. 7 b.   A tree dropping blood into a tub : guarded by a dragon.   62 × 31
10. 9 a.   Two triangular cuts in juxtaposition.
        i. Angel holding a scroll.   60 × 70.
        ii. Man wearing turban in bed.   76 × 72.
11. 10 b.   = FT. 34. [The top line in FT. shews a break only slightly, but
    undoubtedly, indicated here. The apparent difference may perhaps be
    accounted for by the much blacker printing of the cut here. The R. band of
    the Virgin has a break not in FT.]
12. 10 b.   Device No. 2.

3. Van der nieuwer werelt.

The measurements given for Nos. 3 and 4 depend for their correctness on the
    correspondence of the size in the facsimile with that of the original. No. 2
    belongs to the *Oorspronck* set B, and is of much better workmanship than
    the others. No. 1 reappears in the *Reyse van Lissebone* and in the *New
    Lands.*
  1. Fo. 1 a.   Double cut ; the two compartments are at right angles.
        i. A naked man and woman.   ii. Two men, one bearded, and a woman,
        clothed.   (In facsimile 76 × 80 : in NL. 79 × 80.)
  2. 1 b.   **Jonah** thrown to the whale ; arch.   (In facs. 93 × 53 : in O. 97 × 53.)

3. 3 a.   Four naked women, one with a bow.   (80 × 81.)
4. 4 b.   Three savages fighting other three with bows; double lines.   (91 × 76.)
5. 6 a.   Canopus: six stars and 16 S-shaped figures.   No edges.
   6 b.   = No. 1.
6. 7 a.   Canopus: three stars and 16 S-shaped figures.   No edges.
   8 b.   = No. 2.

4. Die reyse van Lissebone.

All these cuts reappear in the *New Lands*.   They seem to be by the same cutter as Nos. 2-4 in the *Van der Nieuwer Werelt*.

1. Fo. 1 a.   Naked family: GENNEA.   68 × 71.
   1 b.   = No. 1.
2. 2 a.   Man, woman and child seated: IN . ALLAGO.   67 × 70.
3. 2 b.   Man and woman; a child between them.   IN. ARABIA.   68 × 80.
4. 3 a.   Similar group: child dances.   MAIOR ; INDIA.   67 × 75.
5. 3 b.   A tree.   66 × 73.
6. 4 a.   Two savages fighting; one has bow, the other shield and sword.   67 × 83.
7. 4 b.   Native chief borne in state on a stretcher.   A large cut without edge lines; placed sideways.   105 × 145.
8. 11 a.   = NW. 1.
9. 12 b.   Device 3 A.

5. Longer accidence.

Last page.   Device No. 3 A.

6. Os facies mentum.

Fo. 1 a.   = FT. 2.

7. Destructie van Troyen.

This edition probably contains the woodcuts used by R. van den Dorpe in his edition of this or another work with the same title, for which see Conway, p. 317-318.   According to the *Bibliophile Belge*, vol. 4, p. 19, the title-page has two cuts in juxtaposition; there are 23 cuts in the text, many repeated from older books; one cut is taken from the *Chevalier délibéré* [Campbell 1083].

8. Robin Hood.

Fo. 1 a.   Robin Hood on horseback.   [In facs. 76 × 92.]   Facsimile in Dickson and Edmond, p. 69.

9. Euryalus and Lucretia.

There is part of a woodcut visible on one of the leaves of the only fragment known, but it is not large enough to give any clue to the subject or its treatment.

12. Den oorspronck onser salicheyt.

In the illustrations of this book several sets of cuts are clearly distinguishable. The first set (called A) are for the most part square and enclosed by double lines. A few, however, have thick single lines : and there are some cuts resembling this set in the following list which are probably the work of another hand: these are Nos. 11, 12, and 217. Set B is of far better work and of French origin. One of the cuts appears in NW., so the set must have long been in the printer's possession. The design in this set is usually arched over. Set C is a set of small cuts, very clumsy and rude. Those representing the ten commandments (Nos. 179 to 190) appear to be by the same hand, though the size differs slightly. A few cuts (Nos. 17, 18, 176) have some points of resemblance to the rest, but are very doubtful.

The greater part of Set A of the *Fifteen Tokens* is repeated here, with two cuts (Nos. 192, 211), which do not appear in that book, unless they are found on the missing leaf 23.

A set of cuts representing events in the life of Antichrist **(Nos. 194 to 198)** appear to be by the same hand as set A. A number of cuts representing the deadly sins as women, apparently belonging to set C (Nos. 226, etc.), are copies, not perhaps at first hand, of those in the *Buch der Sieben Todsünden*, printed by J. Bämler at Augsburg. A very close copy of No. 130 (set C) is found in the 'Walsche Schoelmeester' of Noel de Berlaimont, printed at Antwerp by Hans de Laet in 1545.

Besides these larger sets we find a few odd cuts, and small sets. One of these (Nos. 47, 134, 147, etc.) is a series of half-length figures which look as if they had formed part of a blockbook. Another (Nos. 19, 23, 40) is imitated from the cuts at the top of the pages in the *Biblia pauperum*. These, with two cuts of set B and one of set C, are used in combination with the mottoes and texts to form pages directly copied from the arrangement in the *Biblia pauperum* blockbooks. Another small set consists of the Evangelists' symbols (Nos. 38, 61, 164, 218) and four cuts of saints (Nos. 193, 245 to 247).

1-6. A 1 a. Six cuts representing the six days of creation. Each 56-7 × 45.
7, 8. A 1 a. Two blocks on which the title is cut.
9. A 1 b. Coat of arms with sixteen quarterings, crowned. 57 × 48.
10. A 1 b. 'Nobilis brabancia': Conway, p. 315, no. 23. 131 × 105.
    A 2 a   = No. 1.

A 2 b.   = Nos. 2-5.

A 3 a (1) = No. 6.

11. A 3 b (1).   Adam, Eve and the serpent.   93 × 68.

12. A 4 b (1).   Expulsion from Eden.   92 × 69.

13. A 4 b (2).   Creation of Eve.   [A.]   67 × 65.

14. A 5 b (2).   Adam digs, Eve spins: child.   Town at back.   [A.]   68 × 68.

15. A 6 a (1).   Sacrifice of Cain and Abel; death of Abel.   [A.]   64 × 65.

16. B 1 a (1).   Noah's ark, with dove.   [An old cut, much damaged.]   79 × 68.

17. B 2 a (2).   Man under tree.   To him Angel.   Sheep.   Town at back.   [C?]   60 × 41.

18. B 2 b (2).   Birth of the Virgin.   [As 17.]   57 × 39.

19. B 3 a.   Two merchants [half-length] in conversation under an ornamental arch.   66 × 61.

20. B 3 a.   Two men offer a table to the statue of the Sun.   [A.]   64 × 64.

21. B 3 a.   Jephthah with two attendants cuts off his daughter's head.   [A.]   65 × 65.

22. B 3 a.   The Virgin climbing the temple steps.   [C.]   57 × 44.

23. B 5 a (1).   Marriage of Joseph and Mary.   [A.]   70 × 70.

24. B 5 b.   Like no. 19, but two doctors.   67 × 61.

25. B 5 b.   Temptation of Eve.   [B.]   98 × 54.

26. B 5 b.   Annunciation.   [C.]   56 × 46.

27. B 5 b.   Angel appearing to Gideon.   ·DÑ2 TECṼ · VIRORVM · FORTIS-
SIME.   [B.]   97 × 53.

28. C 1 a (2).   Rebekah gives water to Isaac before city gate.   [A.]   66 × 66.

C 2 a.   = No. 19.

29. C 2 a.   Moses and the burning bush.   [B.]   92 × 59.

30. C 2 a.   Joseph and Mary adore the infant Christ.   [C.]   56 × 46.

31. C 2 a.   Aaron's rod on the altar.   [B.]   96 × 51.

32. C 3 a (2).   Sibyl shews Augustus the vision of the Virgin and Child.   [A.]   67 × 66.

33. C 3 b (2).   Joseph in the stocks dreams of the vine.   [A.]   69 × 67.

34. C 4 a (2).   The Virgin spinning; the Child stands before her.   [C.]   58 × 50.

C 4 b.   = No. 24.

35. C 4 b.   Man presenting a document to David on his throne.   [B.]   98 × 53.

36. C 4 b.   Adoration of the Magi.   [C.]   57 × 46.

37. C 4 b.   Queen of Sheba presents gifts to Solomon.   [B.]   96 × 54.

38. C 5 a (1).   Evangelist's Symbol.   "S matheus."   38 × 28.

39. C 6 a (2).   Solomon on his throne.   [A.]   67 × 67.

40. D 1 a.   Like No. 19, but one is a prince.   67 × 62.

41. D 1 a.   Woman holds child on a seat or altar.   [B.]   97 × 62.

42. D 1 a.   The Presentation in the Temple.   [C.]   56 × 46.

46

43. D 1 a. Samuel given to Eli by his mother. [B.] 97 × 52.
    D 2 b. = No. 19.
44. D 2 b. Isaac sends Jacob (with bow) to Laban. [B.] 97 × 52.
45. D 2 b. The journey into Egypt. [C.] 55 × 45.
46. D 2 b. Michal lets David down through the window. [B.] 97 × 52.
47. E 1 b. Half-length of man in high cap (Archaistic). 43 × 26 to 28.
    E 2 a. = No. 19.
48. E 2 a. Moses seeing the golden calf breaks the tables. [B.] 96 × 53.
49. E 2 a. Men worship the Virgin and child as a statue falls off a pillar. [C.]
        61 × 46.
50. E 2 a. The Philistines bring the ark into Dagon's temple. [B.] 98 × **53**.
    E 4 b. = No. 24.
51. E 4 b. Doeg killing 5 priests. The third in process. [B.] 97 × 53.
52. E 4 b. The slaughter of the innocents. [C.] 56 × 46.
53. E 4 b. Athaliah kills the royal children. [B.] 97 × 52.
54. F 1 a (2). The return from Egypt. [C.] 61 × 48.
55. F 1 a (2). = FT. 35.
    F 1 b. = No. 40.
56. F 1 b. Jacob with his family advancing to meet Esau. [B.] 98 × 53.
    F 1 **b.** = No. 54.
57. F 1 b. David kneeling, harp on ground : God in cloud. [B.] 98 × **52**.
    F 2 2 (1). = No. 38.
    F 3 a. = No. 40.
58. F 3 a. The Egyptians drowned in the Red Sea. [B.] 97 × 52.
59. F 3 a. The baptism of Christ. [C.] 56 × 49.
60. F 3 a. The grapes of Eshcol. [B.] 97 × 52.
61. F 3 b (1). Evang. symbol [as no. 38]. "S marc9." 35 × 26.
62. F 4 b (2). Naaman in Jordan. [A.] 67 × 67.
    G 1 b. = No. 24.
63. G 1 b. Esau (with bow) takes the pottage from Jacob. **[B.]** 97 × 56.
64. G 1 b. Satan tempting Christ. [C.] 61 × 48.
    G 1 b. = No. 11.
65. G 2 b. Bel, Daniel, and the dragon. [A ?] 82 × **72**.
    G 3 b. = No. 19.
66. G 3 b. Elijah revives the widow's son. [B.] 98 × 53.
67. G 3 b. Resurrection of Lazarus. [C.] 61 × 48.
68. **G 3 b.** Elisha recovers the dead. [B.] 98 × 53.
    G 6 b. = No. 40.
69. **G 6 b.** The angels appear to Abraham. [B.] 97 × 54.
70. G 6 b. The Transfiguration. [C.] 62 × 47.
71. G 6 b. Shadrach and the others burning. [B.] 96 × 53.
    H 2 b. = No. 24.
72. H 2 b. Nathan's parable to David. In front a man **prostrate.** [B.]
    97 × 53.

47

73. H 2 b. Mary washes Christ's feet. [C.] 62 × 48.
74. H 2 b. Miriam has leprosy. [B.] 97 × 53.
75. H 4 b (1). King Manasseh in the stocks. [A.] 62 × 67.
    J 1 a. = No. 40.
76. J 1 a. The women greet David carrying Goliath's head. [B.] 98 × 54.
77. J 1 a. Triumphal entry of Christ into Jerusalem. [C.] 62 × 47.
78. J 1 a. The prophets at Jericho acknowledge Elisha. [B.] 97 × 53.
    J 1 b (1). = No. 38.
    J 3 a. = No. 24.
79. J 3 a. Joshua and priests establish altar (Ezra iii. 1). Small window at
        back. Soldiers on left. [B.] 97 × 52.
80. J 3 a. Christ drives the sellers out of the temple. [C.] 62 × 48.
81. J 3 a. Judas Maccabaeus : a man kneels before him. [B.] 96 × 53.
    J 5 a. = No. 19.
82. J 5 a. Messenger announces to Jacob outside a town the death of Joseph.
        [B.] 96 × 53.
83. J 5 a. One man seated and two standing conspire against Christ. [C.]
        61 × 47.
84. J 5 a. Absalom speaking with four men at the gate of Jerusalem. [B.]
        98 × 53.
    J 5 b (1). = No. 38.
    K 1 b. = No. 40.
85. K 1 b. Joseph's brothers sell him to the merchants. [B.] 96 × 52.
86. K 1 b. Judas takes the thirty pieces over the counter. [C.] 56 × 45.
87 K 1 b. Little Joseph shakes hands with Potiphar. [B.] 96 × 53.
    K 3 a. = No. 24.
88. K 3 a. Melchizedek (with chalice) meets Abraham in full armour. [B.]
        97 × 53.
89. K 3 a. The last supper. [C.] 62 × 57.
90. K 3 a. Manna falling and collected. [B.] 97 × 52.
    L 1 a. = No. 19.
91. L 1 a. Michaiah's prophecy to Ahab. M. stands in doorway. [B.]
        98 × 53.
92. L 1 a. Christ's farewell to his disciples, in a pillared hall. Tub and towel
        in front. [C.] 62 × 47.
93. L 1 a. The king of Syria (with drawn sword) asks his servants about Elisha.
        [B.] 96 × 54.
94. L 2 b (2). The agony in the garden. [C.] 62 × 48.
    L 4 a. = No. 24.
95. L 4 a. God and two angels drive the devils down to hell. [B.] 99 × 55.
96. L 4 a. Christ strikes terror into the soldiers. [C.] 66 × 49.
97. L 4 a. The foolish virgins walk between devils and hell's mouth. [B.]
        96 × 52.
98. L 5 a (1). Samson slays the Philistines with the jawbone. [A.] 67 × 66.

99. L 5 b (1). Battle. David (harp on shield) fighting. [A.] 73 × 68.
    L 6 a. = No. 40.
100. L 6 a. Joab stabs Abner in the back. Castle on hill. [B.] 97 × 52.
101. L 6 a. Judas kisses Christ. [C.] 60 × 47.
102. L 6 a. Jonathan enters Ptolemais. Gates closed. Two bodies of soldiers, wall and houses at back. [B.] 96 × 52.
103. M 2 a (1). Christ before Annas (round window). [C.] 62 × 48.
104. M 2 b (2). Christ before Caiaphas (square window). [C.] 62 × 49.
    M 3 b. = No. 24.
105. M 3 b. Jezebel threatens Elijah. [B.] 96 × 52.
106. M 3 b. Christ before Pilate (bearded). [C.] 62 × 47.
107. M 3 b. Half-length figure of Daniel above a gate. In front a king and soldiers. [B.] 98 × 53.
108. M 4 b (1). Christ before Pilate. [A second cut. C.] 62 × 47.
109. N 2 b (1). Christ scourged by two men. [C.] 61 × 49.
110. N 3 b (1). Five people looking to right. Scroll down right side, "Benedic deo et morere." [The design is imperfect.] 91 × 30-32.
111. N 3 b (1). God in cloud. Below, a devil beating a man. [Also imperfect.] 85 × 40.
    N 4 a. = No. 19.
112. N 4 a. A lion kills the boys who mock Elisha. [B.] 98 × 52.
113. N 4 a. Jesus blindfolded and mocked. [C.] 62 × 48.
114. N 4 a. Noah's sons and their father's nakedness. [B.] 96 × 52.
115. N 5 b (1). Samson pulling down the pillar supporting the upper story of a building. [A.] 67 × 67.
116. N 6 a (2). Christ mocked. Below : ·: ECCE : ·: HOMO : [C.] 61 × 48.
117. N 6 b (1). Pilate washes his hands. [C.] 61 × 48.
    O 2 a. = No. 24.
118. O 2 a. Abraham and Isaac journeying to Moriah. [B.] 98 × 54.
119. O 2 a. Christ falls under the cross. [C.] 61 × 47.
120. O 2 a. Widow with two logs stands before priest in chair holding a book. [B.] 96 × 52.
121. O 4 b (1). Christ stript of the purple robe. [C.] 62 × 48.
122. O 4 b (2). Christ nailed to the cross. [C.] 61 × 48.
123. P 1 a (1). The two vinedressers kill the heir. [A.] 68 × 68.
    P 1 b. = No. 19.
124. P 1 b. The sacrifice of Isaac. [B.]
125. P 1 b. Crucifixion (one cross, Mary and John). [C.] 62 × 47.
126. P 1 b. The Brazen Serpent. [B.] 98 × 53.
127. P 3 b (1). The king of Moab kills his son. [A.] 68 × 66.
128. P 4 b (2). Crucifixion (3 crosses). [C ?] 56 × 48.
    P 5 a. = No. 40.
129. P 5 a. Creation of Eve. [B.] 97 × 53.
130. P 5 a. Christ's side pierced by a soldier. [C.] 53 × 46.

131. P 5 a. Moses strikes the rock. [B.] 97 × 52.
132. P 6 b (1). Absalom **hanging** in a tree. Two men spear him. [A.]
68 × 67.
133. Q 1 b. Small archaic cut. [From a blockbook?] Man in front of wall
    with **two** windows holding a scroll on which is "Sentio".
    33 × 25·26.
134. Q 1 b. Similar cut to No. 47, in a turban. 39 × **28.**
135. Q 1 b. Descent from T-cross. [C.] 61 × 48.
136. Q 1 b. Adam and Eve mourning for Abel. [A.] 62 × 65.
137. Q 1 b. **City** at back. A woman (Naomi) weeping over two corpses. [A.]
68 × 65.
      Q 2 b. = No. 19.
138. Q 2 b. Joseph drawn out of the **well** by his **brothers.** [B.] **97** × 55.
139. Q 2 b. Christ laid in tomb. [C.] 62 × 47.
140. Q 2 b. = NW No. 2. [B.]
      Q 3 b. = No. 19.
141. Q 3 b. David kills **Goliath.** [B.] 96 × 52.
142. Q 3 b. Christ draws the spirits out of hell's mouth. [C.] 61 × **47.**
143. Q 3 b. Samson slays the lion. [B.] 97 × 52.
144. R 1 b (1). Ahud kills Eglon. [A.] 67 × 66.
145. R 2 a (1). Man in **flames. 3** others astonished. God above. [A.]
66 × 66.
146. R 2 a (2). Large bird brings a **snake to another** in a bottle. [A.]
68 × 67.
      R 2 b. = No. 134.
147. R 2 b. **Another** figure like No. 47; large hat, long beard. 40 × 27.
148. R 2 b. A **female** saint with crown and halo standing on a devil, holding
    and surrounded by **the instruments** of the passion. [A.]
67 × 67.
149. R 2 b. Jael driving nail into Sisera's head. [A.] 66 × 66.
150. R 2 b. Judith holding the head of Holofernes, who is in bed. [A.]
67 × 67.
      R 5 a. = No. 40.
151. R 5 a. Jonah emitted by whale. **[B.] 98 × 54.**
152. R 5 a. The resurrection. [C.] 61 × **46.**
153. R 5 a. Samson carrying the gates of Gaza. **[B.] 96 × 53.**
      R 5 b (1). = No. 61.
      R 6 a. = No. 24.
154. R 6 a. Reuben at the well looking for Joseph. [B.] 93 × 53.
155. R 6 a. Angels and women at the empty tomb. [C.] 61 × 47.
156. R 6 a. Woman weeping. Scroll down right side; legend, in French
    (woodcut) characters: Quesiui iesum et non inueni. Ca. iii.
    [B.] 95 × 53.
      S 1 b. = No. 19.

157. S 1 b. Daniel in lion's den. King at the door. [B.] 97 × 53.
158. S 1 b. Christ appears to Magdalen. [C.] 62 × 46.
159. S 1 b. Christ and a maiden. Above a scroll bearing in letters of a French
            form : Tenui eū nec demittā. can. iii. [B.] 98 × 54.
160. T 2 b (2). A doctor preaching in a church. [C ?] 55 × 66.
    V 4 b (1). = No. 160.
    V 5 a (2). = No. 160.
    X 2 b. = No. 40.
161. X 2 b. Meeting of Jacob and Joseph. A child in front. [B.] **97 × 52.**
162. X 2 b. The supper at Emmaus. [C.] 62 × 48.
163. X 2 b. Return of the prodigal son. [B.] 96 × 53.
164. X 3 a. Evangelist's symbol, "lucas" (as no. 38). 38 × 29.
    X 4 b. = No. 40.
165. X 4 b. Gideon speaking with an angel. [B.] 97 × 52.
166. X 4 b. Thomas puts his hand into Christ's side. [C.] 62 × 48.
167. **X** 4 b. Jacob wrestling with the angel. [B.] 97 × 53.
    AA 1 a. = No. 19.
168. AA 1 a. Enoch lifted into heaven. [B.] 97 × 53.
169. AA 1 a. The ascension. [C.] 61 × 47.
170. AA 1 a. Elijah going up in a waggon. Elisha **kneels** below. **[B.]**
            96 × 50.
    AA 2 b. = No. 40.
171. AA 2 b. Moses receiving the tables. [B.] 97 × **51.**
172. AA 2 b. Descent of the holy Ghost. [C.] 62 × 48.
173. AA 2 b. Elijah's sacrifice takes fire. [B.] 97 × 52.
174. BB 4 b. Elisha and many barrels of oil. [A.] 66 × 66.
    CC 1 a. = No. 19.
175. CC 1 a. Esther and Ahasuerus. Below, 2 gallows. [B.] 97 × 53.
176. CC 1 a. Christ crowning the Virgin. [As 17 ?] 41 × 36.
177. CC 1 a. Solomon seats Bathsheba by his side. [B.] 96 × 52.
178. CC 3 b. Moses holding the two tablets, which bear inscriptions in type 1.
            Above his head, and down his front on a long scroll, are inscrip-
            tions in type 2 (the commandments). 247 × 105.
179. CC 4 a (2). Moses receiving the tables. [C.] 57 × 43.
180. CC 4 a (2). Side piece. Moses holding the tables. [C.] 57 × 24.
181. CC 5 a (1). Two men gambling and swearing. [C.] 57 × 44.
182. CC 5 a (1). Side piece like 180. [C.] 59 × 25.
183. CC 5 a (2). Priest elevating the Host. [C.] 56 × 44.
    CC 5 a (2). = No. 180.
184. CC 5 b (2). Two children and their parents. [C.] 57 × 44.
    CC 5 b (2). = No. 182.
185. CC 6 a (1). Man with sword grasps hair of one with dagger. **[C.]**
            57 × 44.
    CC 6 a (1). = No. 180.

186. CC 6 b (1). Man in bed : another carries off his purse. [C.] 57 × 44.
     CC 6 b (1). = No. 180.
187. CC 6 b (2). In a wood, a woman sits on a man's knee. [C.] 51 × 45.
188. DD 1 b (1). Two men before a judge. One raises his left arm. [C.]
                 57 × 43.
     DD 1 b (1). = No. 180.
189. DD 2 a (2). A man tempts a woman with coin. [C.] 57 × 45.
     DD 2 a (2). = No. 182.
190. DD 2 b (2). One man coveting another's money. [C.] 57 × 44.
     DD 2 b (2). = No. 182.
     DD 4 a (1). = No. 160.
191. EE 1 a (1). Man in bed : Death at foot, angels at head : a priest and a devil
                 at sides. 97 × 84.
192. EE 5 a (2). The seven mercies of God [as FT. set A]. 83 × 62.
193. EE 5 b (1). Small cut of saint holding book [as no. 38 ?] 34 × 24.
194. EE 6 a (1). Antichrist as a priest. [A.] 65 × 64.
195. EE 6 a (2). Antichrist judging three men. [A.] 67 × 65.
196. EE 6 b (1). Antichrist as a king, with four lords. [A.] 68 × 65.
197. EE 6 b (2). Antichrist preaching over two dead saints. [A.] 66 × 66.
198. FF 1 a (1). Antichrist, as cardinal, slaying kings. [A.] 70 × 66.
199. FF 1 b (1). = FT. 3.
200. FF 1 b (1). = FT. 4.
201. FF 2 a (1). = FT. 5.
202. FF 2 a (1). = FT. 6.
203. FF 2 b (1). = FT. 7.
204. FF 2 b (1). = FT. 8.
205. FF 3 a (1). = FT. 9.
206. FF 3 a (1). = FT. 10.
207. FF 3 b (1). = FT. 11.
208. FF 3 b (1). = FT. 1.
209. FF 4 a (1). = FT. 12.
210. FF 4 b (1). = FT. 14.
211. FF 4 b (1). Heaven and earth in flames [same set]. 65 × 74.
212. GG 1 a (1). = FT. 15.
     GG 2 a. = No. 24.
213. GG 2 a. David has the youth who claims to have slain Saul killed. [B.]
             97 × 51.
214. GG 2 a. The last judgment. [C.] 61 × 47.
215. GG 2 a. The judgment of Solomon. [B.] 95 × 52.
216. GG 3 b (2). = FT. 16. [A.]
217. HH 4 b (1). The five chief devils. 64 × 76.
     JJ 1 a (1). = No. 47.
     JJ 1 a (2). = No. 134.
     JJ 1 b (1). = No. 147.

218. JJ 1 b (2). Evang. symbol "S Johēs" [as 38]. **37 × 27.**
 JJ 2 a (1). = No. 147.
 JJ 2 a (2). = No. 47.
 JJ 2 b (1). = No. 147.
 JJ 2 b (2). = No. 47.
 JJ 3 a (1). = No. 47.
 JJ 3 a (2). = No. 147.
 JJ 3 b (1). = No. 218.
219. JJ 4 a (2). King facing left [as 47]. **43 × 28.** .
 JJ 4 b (1). = No. 134.
 KK 1 a. = No. 40.
220. KK 1 a. Destruction of Sodom and Gomorrah by fire from heaven. **[B.]**
 96 × 53.
221. **KK 1 a.** Two devils torturing souls in hell. [C.] 56 × 44.
222. **KK 1 a.** Cities and men destroyed together by earthquake. **[B.]**
 96 × 52.
223. KK 2 b. Lot and others with an angel: Lot's **wife** looks back. **[A.]**
 66 × 66.
224. KK 6 b (1). Souls in purgatory. Blank scroll. **Angel** above. [C?]
 49 × 40.
 KK 6 b (1). = No. 55.
 LL 2 a (2). = No. 160.
225. **LL** 3 b. "Ymago peccati mortalis", **with two scrolls filled with type 2.**
 82 × 82.
226. **LL** 4 b **(2).** Woman **on** horse holding mirror. *Hovnerdicheyt.* **[C.]**
 55 × 45.
227. **MM** 2 a (1). Christ in **robe** and crown. Two men with stick twist
 crown. [Cf. FT. 38. C.] 62 × 47.
228. MM 2 a (1). Angel holding soul before him (side piece). [C.] 56 × **32.**
229. **MM** 2 a (1). Devils torturing souls on wheels. [C.] 57 × 44.
230. **MM** 2 b (1). Woman on mule with a bone in its mouth. *Nidicheyt.* [C.]
 56 × 44.
231. **MM** 3 b (2). Another cut like No. 228. **54 × 23.**
 MM 3 b (2). = No. 221.
 MM 4 a (1). = No. 130.
232. MM 4 a (1). Old man leaning on stick (a side piece). **47 × 19.**
233. **MM** 4 a (2). Women with sword riding on a bear. *Toernicheyt.* **[C.]**
 56 × 45.
 NN 1 a (1). = No. 231.
234. NN 1 a (1). = Two devils hacking souls with swords. **[C.]** 56 × 45.
 NN 1 a (1). = No. 109.
235. NN 1 a (2). Woman seated on a toad, holding a jug. *Ghiesicheyt.* [C.]
 56 × 45.
 NN 2 a (1). = No. 231.

236. NN 2 a (1). = Devils boiling souls in a caldron. [C.] 57 × 43.
    NN 2 a (1). = No. 232.
    NN 2 a (1). = No. 121
237. NN 2 a (2). Man seated on donkey. *Traechz.* [C.] 57 × 45.
    NN 3 a (1). = No. 228.
238. NN 3 a (1). Two devils shooting arrows at souls. [C.] 57 × 44.
    NN 3 a (1). = No. 232.
    NN 3 a (1). = No. 122.
239. NN 3 a (2). Woman on a hog holding a goblet. *Gulsicheyt.* [C.]
        57 × 44.
    NN 3 b (2). = No. 231.
240. NN 4 a (1). Devils make souls eat snakes. [C.] 57 × 44.
    NN 4 a (1). = No. 232.
    NN 4 a (1). = No. 94.
241. NN 4 a (2). Woman on **goat embraced by man.** *Luxurien.* [C.]
        56 × 45.
    NN 5 b (1). = No. 157.
242. NN 5 b (1). Soul forced by a devil into a sulphur lake full of monsters
        [cut broken. C.] 57 × 44.
243. NN 5 b (2). Circumcision of Christ [has not occurred before. C.]
        62 × 48.
244. OO 1 a (2). Confession, under floriated arch. 65 × 42.
245-247. OO 2 b (2). Three cuts of SS. Gregory, Ambrose, Augustine [as
        No. 193]. 38 × 27, 37 × 26.
    OO 3 a. = No. 40.
248. OO 3 a. Job and family at table under a canopy. [B.] 96 × 51.
249. OO 3 a. Christ holding souls in a sheet. [C.] 61 × 45.
250. OO 3 a. The banquet of Ahasuerus. [B.] 96 × 51.
251. PP 1 a. Jacob's dream. Two angels on the ladder. [A.] 64 × 65.
    PP 2 a. = No. 24.
252. PP 2 a. A king crowning his bride (Cantica). [B.] 97 × 52.
253. PP 2 a. Christ crowning his bride. [C.] 62 × 46.
254. PP 2 a. Angel speaking to S. John. [B.] 97 × 52.
255. QQ 4 b. Device 3 B.

14. Letter of B. de Clereville.

No. 1 is an imitation of the *Chronicle* series, and is used in the edition of 1512
    printed by H. Eckert. A copy of this cut is used on fo. 99 b of the Dutch
Bible printed by Claes de Grave, 28 June 1518. The copy is much
damaged. That it is a copy and not the original seems clear from the fact
that a slightly smaller size is obtained by omitting part of the design round
the edge. Nos. 2-4 appear to belong to one set.

1. 1 a. A battle. One army retreats to the right behind rocks ; a horseman bearing a bird on his shield is unhorsed. The other army advances ; the leader, a lion on his shield, brandishes a sword. 103 × 102.

2. 1 b. A man with a spear gives a letter to a youth in a doorway. 69 × 51.

3. 3 b. A man with long hair carrying a letter, lifts his hat. A fox's brush hangs down his back. 70 × 50.

4. 3 b. A Pope with triple cross and **crown blesses.** **72 × 28.**

15. **Brabant** Chronicle.

This edition (Conway, p. 314) contains the set of *Chronicle* cuts first used by R. van den Dorpe in 1497, and again by Eckert in 1512. It is probable that most of the additional cuts found in the edition of 1530 (see below) are not employed here.

16. Virgilius.

Nos. 1, 5, 6, 7, 8, 9 appear to belong to one **set, whether** cut for **this edition or** not it is difficult to say. They are **perhaps by** the same **hand as Nos. 3** and 13. The rest are chiefly odd cuts. **Nos.** 3 and **13 belong to the** *Oorspronck* set A. No. 4 seems to be German work. **Nos. 1, 5, 6, 7, 11** are copied in the Dutch edition printed by Vorsterman.

1. Fo. 1 a. The Romans lighting their candles. [A.] 83 × 65.

2. 2 b. Romulus riding into the town of Reynes. 127 × 83.

3. 3 b. = O. 144.

4. 5 a. Schoolmaster and three pupils : branches above. 118 × 87.

5. 7 b. Virgilius speaking with the Emperor. [A.] 86 × 51.

6. 11 b. V. hanging in a basket and mocked by women. [A.] 83 × 64.
   13 a. = No. 1.

7. 14 a. Statue of Rome surrounded by the gods, on a pillar. [A.] 87 × **50.**

8. 17 b. Two men planting trees. [A.] 65 × 64.

9. 19 b. V. carrying off the Soldan's daughter. [A.] **81 × 69.**

10. 20 b. The Soldan and his attendants, one in black. **72 × 51.**

11. 20 b. Woman in bed, in a turban. 70 × 32.

12. 21 b. V. bound and carried off by two men. 96 **× 88.**

13. 22 b. Two workmen building a tower. 67 × 67.

14. 25 b. Two snakes : one has a head at each end. 83 × 58. [= DP. 23.]

15. 30 a. The arms of England crowned. 71 × 48.

16. 30 b. Device 3 a.

17. Frederick of Jennen.

Several of the cuts [A.] in this book are quite distinct from those in any other of J. van Doesborgh's productions. The work is fine, and detail is greatly insisted **on.** Of the rest those marked [B.] seem to belong together. The **rest are** doubtful. One, No. 3, belongs to the *Parson of Kalenborowe* set. No. 24 is copied in the Dutch *Virgilius* printed by Vorsterman. Nos. 8, 11, 13, 20, 21, 23 are copied in the English edition printed by A. Vele.

1. Fo. 1 a. Frederick in armour, standing. 92 × 68.
2. 1 b. = V. 15.
3. 2 b. Two men on horseback. [B.] 70 × 49.
4. 2 b. Man on horseback, in black cloak. [B.] 70 × 39.
5. 4 a. Youth in pointed shoes, standing outside a door. 65 × 40.
6. 4 a. Man seated on bench, holding out hand. [As 5?] 65 × 40.
7. 6 a. Man issuing from house on left. [A.] 68 × 55.
8. 6 a. Two nuns. [As 5?] 68 × 42.
9. 7 a. A man hands a robe to a woman standing by a coffer, in a square. [A.] 68 × 100.
10. 8 b. Old woman greeting young one in open space. A dog lying on the ground. [A.] 68 × 87.
11. 9 b. Two men hauling a chest on a wheelbarrow towards a woman standing in doorway. [A.] 69 × 93.
    10 b. = No. 7.
12. 10 b. = V. 11. [B.]
    12 b. = No. 4.
13. 13 a. A man killing a dog in a wood. [A.] 70 × 51.
14. 13 a. Woman clasping her hands. [B.] 70 × 35.
15. 14 a. Three persons in a boat under sail. 70 × 51.
16. 14 a. Man girt with sword holds a stick in his left hand, extends the right. [B.] 70 × 36.
17. 15 a. = DP. 181.
18. 16 a. = L. 1.
19. 17 a. Two men in long gowns [very bad : as No. 3 ?] 66 × 30.
20. 17 a. Merchant opening his pack. [B.] 71 × 36.
21. 18 b. = L. 2.
22. 20 b. = V. 10. [B.]
23. 20 b. A naked woman. [B.] 69 × 36.
24. 22 b. King with a favourite who whispers to him, and two attendants. 68 × 47.
25. 22 b. Woman standing on chequered floor in attitude of supplication. [B.] 67 × 34.
26. 24 b. Device 3 B.
    25 a. = No. 2.
    25 b. = No. 26.

18. Mary of Nemmegen.

Of the cuts in this book, all except Nos. 5, 6, 12, 13 belong to a single set, and are certainly above the average of the illustrations used by our printer. The surrounding line is double, connected at the corners by short **diagonal** lines.

1. Fo. 1 a.   The devil appears to Mary as she sits under the hedge.   86 × **83.**
2. 1 b.   Mary taking leave of her uncle.   87 × 84.
3. 3 a.   Mary taking leave of her aunt; a copy of No. 2.   88 × 83.
   3 b.   = No. 1.
4. 7 a.   The aunt kills herself.   Her soul borne off by two devils.   88 × **84.**
5. 10 b.   = FJ. 5.
6. 10 b.   = FJ. 25.
7. 12 b.   The devil carrying Mary through the air to her uncle.   88 × **86.**
8. 14 a.   Mary lying at foot of wall; the devil speaks to her uncle.   88 × **84.**
9. 14 b.   Mary and her uncle, with pix, setting out.   The devil above.
   87 × 84.
10. 15 b.   Mary and the pope, in two scenes.   87 × 88.
11. 18 b.   Mary asleep.   An angel removes the rings.   **88 × 88.**
12. 20 a.   = V. 15.
13. 20 b.   Device 3 a.

19. Howleglas.

The existing fragment has only one cut, doubtless one of a set.   **It is a rude** performance, without any attempt at a background.

J4 a.   Howleglas hands the pot to the winedrawer at Lübeck.   **78 × 63.**

20. Thuys der fortunen.

This book contains cuts.   There is no doubt that the six cuts entitled 'The house of death' in DP. and WS. are reproductions of pages in this edition: the two cuts representing the ages of man and the corresponding animals very probably also come from the same source.

21. Der **dieren** palleys.

With a few exceptions the cuts in this book belong to a single set.   These are all more or less bad, the majority execrable, a few atrocious, one or two, especially those which look like illustrations to Aesop (Nos. 163, 164), almost tolerable.   That they were not designed for this particular edition is shown by their broken condition, and by the fact that at least one belonged to J. van Doesborgh in 1518 (FJ. no. 17).   Another occurs at about the same date in *Virgilius*.   The rest of the cuts are chiefly apospasmatia.   Those marked B (Nos. 37, 39, 48, 66) belong to the curious archaistic set which occurs in the *Oorspronck*.   Those (Nos. 169 *sqq.*) called C are apparently by the same hand as set B in the *Fifteen Tokens*.   Those cuts which do not belong to any set in particular are called A.   Some of these are noticeable : Nos. 9 to 14, and possibly 5, 6, 8, 15, 168, as being cuts from the book called *Thuys der fortunen*. No. 7 is an old fifteenth-century cut, which came from Delft to Antwerp with H. Eckert. No. 126 is particularly interesting, as being one of the set used in the *Nieuwer Werelt*, but not found in any of Doesborgh's known American books: compare *New lands*, No. 1 No. 137 is very curious, and it is difficult to conjecture its source: the work is very good. No. 199 is apparently from a devotional book. Those cuts which reappear in NL. are all in a better state here, and help to fix a date for that work. There are also two cuts taken from the *Fifteen Tokens*, and one from the *Oorspronck* set A.

1. **A 1 a.** Birds, beasts and fishes. At top three figures. [A.] **245 × 169.**
2. **A 1 a.** Two blocks on which part of the title is cut. [A.]
3. **A 1 b.** Prince's portrait under arch, with quarterings. [A.] **124 × 93.**
4. **A 2 a.** = O. 13.
5. **A 3 b and 4 a.** The ten ages of man (one block). [A.] **354 × 73.**
6. **A 3 b and 4 a.** The ten corresponding animals (one block). [A.] **354 × 33.**
7. **A 4 b.** S. Augustine: **Conway,** p. 278, no. 46: heart inked in. [A.] **77 × 38.**
8. **A 5 a.** Anatomical figure [A.] **121 × 90.**
9. **A 5 b.** Death enthroned. [A.] **72 × 47.**
10. **A 5 b.** Skeletons. [A.] **46 × 57.**
11. **A 5 b.** Colericus. [A.] 70 × 47.
12. **A 5 b.** Flegmaticus. [A.] 71 × 48.
13. **A 5 b.** Sanguineus. [A.] 70 × 48.
14. **A 5 b.** Melancholicus. [A.] 71 × 48.
15. **A 6 b.** Phrenological head. [A.] **121 × 92.**
16. **B 1 a (2).** Shepherd and four lambs. **56 × 63.**
17. **B 1 b (2).** Two rams. **59 × 64.**
18. **B 2 a (2).** Two boars. **68 × 61**
19. **B 3 a (1).** Ass. **73 × 63.**
20. **B 3 b (2).** Two animals: one, like an ox, walks downwards: the other has circular small serrated horns. **82 × 62.**
21. **B 4 a (1).** Four animals: two facing right, two left: one is a goat. **81 × 62.**
22. **B 4 b (1).** Two snakes swimming below willows. **81 × 57.**
23. **B 4 b (2).** = V. 14.
24. **B 5 a (1).** Three asps attacking a prostrate man. **54 × 64.**
25. **B 5 b (1).** Spider in her web. **54 × 63.**
26. **B 5 b (2).** Two snaily animals. **54 × 62.**
27. **B 6 a (1).** 'Bonnacon.' 3 legs. One horn outside cut at top. **82 × 60.**
28. **B 6 a (2).** Ox. **81 × 62.**
29. **C 1 a (1).** Silkworm. **42 × 63.**
30. **C 1 a (2).** Two 'boraxes' (toads). **82 × 64.**
31. **C 1 b (2).** Three toads. **49 × 64.**
32. **C 2 a (2).** Two buffaloes, with serrated horns. **80 × 65.**

33. C 2 b (1).   Three grasshoppers. 71 × 57.
34. C 2 b (2).   'Buprestis': like a bull. 83 × 58.
35. C 3 a (1).   Four flies hovering round a cask. 46 × 65.
36. C 3 a (2).   Goat. 83 × 56.
37. C 3 b (1).   Half length figure of man in gown. Nearly a quarter of the
                  block is left blank. [B.] 37 × 28.
38. C 3 b (2).   Stonebuck; with drooping ears. 61 × 58.
39. C 4 a (1).   = O. 47. [B.]
40. C 4 a (2).   Five dogs. 82 × 65.
    C 4 b (2).   = No. 37.
41. D 1 a (1).   Two cats at a fountain. 68 × 59.
42. D 1 b (1).   'Caccus'; breathing fire. 82 × 64.
43. D 1 b (2).   Camel. 81 × 63.
    D 2 a (2).   = No. 39.
44. D 2 b (1).   'Cameleon.' Long neck and tail: one forepaw raised. 80 × 65.
    D 2 b (2).   = No. 37.
45. D 3 a (1).   'Cameleō.' A hairy camel. 80 × 64.
46. D 3 a (2).   'Capriolus.' 75 × 63.
47. D 3 b (1).   Beaver with a branch. 79 × 63.
48. D 4 a (1).   Half-length figure in a turban. [B.]. 40 × 26.
49. D 4 b (1).   Man teaching 'chama' to stand on its hind legs. 81 × 57.
50. D 4 b (2).   'Calopus.' 80 × 60.
51. E 1 a (1).   The hart, drinking. 69 × 64.
52. E 1 b (2).   'Zilio' killing a man. 81 × 64.
53. E 2 a (1).   'Cecula'; snakes under trees.
54. E 2 a (2).   'Cerastes,' with eight horns. 81 × 63.
55. E 2 b (1).   'Cephos' and 'Centrocota'; two monsters. 73 × 63.
56. E 2 b (2).   'Cirogrillus'; like a pig. 43 × 59.
57. E 2 b (2).   'Crekelen': four beetles. 43 × 57.
58. E 3 a (1).   'Cycotrocea': toed animal with head like a cat. 57 × 61.
59. E 3 a (2).   'Critetus'; like a puppy: fills only half the space. 33 × 62.
60. E 3 b (1).   'Coluber'; several curling snakes. 46 × 63.
61. E 3 b (2).   'Cocodrillus' jumping: castle at back. 73 × 66.
62. E 4 a (2).   Four coneys. 62 × 61.
63. E 4 b (1).   'Damma'; has horns with gouttes. 70 × 58.
64. F 1 a (1).   'Damula'; like a goat. 74 × 65.
65. F 1 a (2).   Dragon. 87 × 66.
66. F 1 b (1).   Like O. 133, but a different block. [B.]. 39 × 28.
67. F 1 b (2).   'Draconcopedes': serpent with woman's head. 68 × 64.
68. F 2 a (2).   'Dasse': a pig with sharp snout. 55 × 70.
69. F 2 a (2).   'Dypsa.' A man drinking, and 3 snakes. 70 × 63.
70. F 2 b (1).   'Dromeda' and 'dammula.' 83 × 64.
    F 2 b (2).   = No. 39.
71. F 3 a (1).   Man with sword fighting the hydra. 76 × 56.

72. **F 3 a (2).** The horse. 80 × 63.
　　F 3 b (1). = No. 37.
73. **F 3 b (2).** Elephant : standing on his trunk. 73 × 63.
　　F 4 b (1). = No. 39.
74. **F 4 b (1).** 'Enchires.' One horn shaded, one white. 81 × 58.
75. **F 4 b (2).** 'Enidros.' Two, one has saw-like tail held up. 57 × 61.
76. **G 1 a (1).** 'Cyrogrillus' and 'Erinacius': one a pig, the other holds a lizard. 51 × 63.
77. **G 1 a (2).** 'Edus.' Two ; one stands on its hind legs. 43 × 63.
78. **G 1 b (1).** 'Emorrois.' Three snakes, one three-headed. 76 × 64.
79. **G 1 b (2).** A tree and a leech. 63 × 58.
80. **G 2 a (1).** 'Falena' and 'Fiber,' resembling a boar and a sheep. 71 × 63.
81. **G 2 a (2).** Four ants on and about a tree-trunk. 70 × 59.
82. **G 2 b (1).** 'Myren.' Toed animal with a bulbous body. 35 × 56.
83. **G 3 a (1).** 'Furus' and 'Furunculus.' One is a six-legged beetle. 57 × 57.
84. **G 3 a (2).** Gazelle, with horns and tusks, leaping. 78 × 63.
85. **G 3 b (1).** 'Gamaleon '; quadruped with wings and long tail. 72 × 66.
86. **G 4 a (1).** 'Glandosa' and 'Gnatrix': two snakes, one in cistern ; the other kills a man. 78 × 58.
87. **G 4 a (2).** 'Grillus' : a sharp-nosed, six-legged beetle. 29 × 62.
88. **G 4 b (1).** 'Hericeus.' Three hedgehogs or urchins. 46 × 62.
　　G 4 b (1). = No. 37.
89. **G 4 b (2).** 'Hirena' or hyaena. 58 × 58.
90. **H 1 a (1).** 'Histrix': very like No. 56. 44 × 57.
91. **H 1 a (2).** The buck. Hairy back and indented curved horns. 69 × 57.
92. **H 1 b (2).** 'Hinnulus '; walking downhill, with one foreleg raised. 75 × 61.
93. **H 2 a (1).** 'Jaculus.' Man under tree attacked by winged snake. 81 × 62.
94. **H 2 a (2).** 'Icinus.' Two, resembling guinea-pigs. 44 × 71.
95. **H 2 b (1).** Two lizards. 58 × 70.
96. **H 2 b (2).** 'Lamia' and 'Lausanum '; ox and goat. 80 × 57.
97. **H 3 a (1).** Two lions. 79 × 63.
98. **H 3 b (1).** Leopard seated. 67 × 58.
99. **H 3 b (2).** 'Leonthophorus,' like a lion, and 'Leucrocuta.' 78 × 64.
100. **H 4 a (1).** Hare leaping among rocks. 71 × 59.
　　H 4 b (2). = No. 65. Here 'Leviathan.'
101. **J 1 a (1).** Silkworm (snail) and cocoon. 59 × 62.
　　J 1 b (1). = No. 58. Here 'Lintworm.'
　　J 1 b (2). = No. 33.
102. **J 2 a (1).** Three wolves howling over their prey. 70 × 57.
103. **J 2 b (1).** 'Luter' holding a fish.
104. **J 2 b (2).** A man shiting worms. 59 × 40.
105. **J 3 a (1).** 'Lichaon ': calf-like, three-toed animal. 50 × 61.

106. J 3 a (2). 'Maricomorion.' Quadruped with human head and long tail. 72 × 62.
107. J 3 b (1). Weasel, a small animal. 32 × 58.
108. J 3 b (2). 'Mumumetus,' with human head, and 'Manticora,' a monkey. 80 × 58.
109. J 4 a (1). 'Marter'; small animal under a tree. 55 × 64.
110. J 4 a (2). 'Melois,' 'Melosus,' 'Monocheros,' and a child. 80 × 61.
111. J 4 b (1). 'Migale,' like No. 107, but the back touches top of **cut**. 31 × 58.
    J 4 b (2). Mule. = No. 19.
112. K 1 a (1). Two black mice. 39 × 61.
113. K 1 b (1). 'Musquelibet,' letting his "impostume" run out. 74 × 64.
114. K 1 b (2). 'Daer' or multipes. Five crawling about a stone. 49 × 62.
115. K 1 b (2). 'Nepa.' Two spotted snakes : one's head is dropping **off**. 48 × 67.
116. K 2 a (1). 'Neomon': a lizard fighting a snake. 46 × **59.**
117. K 2 a (2). Three wild asses. 82 × 61.
118. K 2 b (1). 'Orafflus' (giraffe) and 'Onocenthaurus,' **man** with ass's head, holding a staff. 81 × 62.
    K 2 b (2). = No. 116 upside down.
    K 3 a (1). 'Orix.' = No. 91.
119. K 3 a (2). Panther, with large spots, breathing fire. **67** × 62.
    K 3 b (1). 'Papro.' = No. 102.
120. K 3 b (2). 'Pathion.' Three sheeplike animals marked with stars. 57 × 65.
121. K 4 a (1). 'Parandrus,' a stag ; and 'Pardus,' spotted and leaping. 81 × 58.
122. K 4 a (2). 'Pilosus,' etc. Man with animal's hindquarters ; small animal with hairy mouth. 74 × 57.
123. **K** 4 b (1). = PJ. 1, with a worm-hole.
124. K 4 b (2). 'Pegasius'; a winged cow. 74 × 66.
125. L 1 a (1). 'Pigargus,' a goat with long horns. 72 × **62.**
126. L 1 a (2). Two Indians point spears at birds' **nests in trees.** [A.] 89 × 68.
127. **L** 1 b (1). 'Vuellen'; like sheep: one large and two **small ones.** **84** × 58.
128. **L 2 a** (1). A bed with two pillows and four huge fleas. **58** × **57.**
    L 2 a (1). = No. 37.
    L 2 a (1). = No. 48.
129. **L 2 b** (1). Two boars fighting before an oak tree. 82 × 63.
130. **L 2 b** (2). 'Pader'; snakes. One raises itself to top of cut. 75 × 55.
131. L 3 a (1). Two frogs on a striped ground. 57 × 63.
132. L 3 a (2). 'Rangifer,' with 3 long and 2 short horns : below, a squirrel. 79 × 58.
    L 3 b (2). = No. 112.

133. L 4 a (1).   'Regulus': cock with snake's tail. 72 × 62.
134. L 4 a (2).   'Rutela': spider and web between trees. 60 × 58.
135. L 4 b (1).   Salamander in flames. 62 × 58.
136. L 4 b (2).   'Saura' like a small seal, with long spiral tail: stars along
                  body. 36 × 59.
137. M 1 a (1).   Man in fool's cap sits at table, on to which a cat climbs.
                  Label: Soudie mij met drincken ver ‖ ghetē Die kat ſou
                  mÿ pēſen eten. [A.] 123 × 65.
138. M 1 a (2).   'Ethele'; worms swimming, etc. 36 × 61.
139. M 1 b (1).   'Scrabones,' flies attacking a cow. 51 × 63.
140. M 1 b (2).   'Salpiga,' etc. Three snakes. One bites a man lying who
                  raises his arm. 82 × 63.
141. M 2 a (1).   'Situla,' etc. Three snakes, one winged. 79 × 62.
142. M 2 a (2).   Scorpion, like a four-legged fish: long tail with sting.
                  59 × 38.
143. M 2 b (1).   'Seta.' Three insects: a snake coming out of a hole, and
                  another snake. 57 × 64.
144. M 2 b (2).   'Sploator colubri.' Three six-legged beetles. 61 × 58.
145. M 3 a (1).   Two black moles. 54 × 63.
146. M 3 a (2).   'Stier'; very like Nos. 27, 28. 81 × 59.
     M 3 b (1).   = No. 37.
     M 3 b (1).   = No. 48.
     M 3 b (2).   = No. 74.
147. M 4 a (1).   'Taxus,' a small doglike animal. 29 × 62.
148. M 4 a (2).   'Tragelaphus' and 'Tragodita,' with indented horns. 78 × 66.
149. M 4 b (1).   'Houtworm'; men operating on a tree. 60 × 63.
150. M 4 b (2).   'Motte' woman seated behind table on which are moth-
                  eaten garments. 74 × 65.
151. N 1 a (1).   'Beynocheros' breathing fire. 'Monocheros,' an unicorn.
                  82 × 62.
152. N 1 a (2).   Woman brushing lice out of a man's hair. 79 × 64.
153. N 1 b (1).   'Tirus': tree with nest; man seated at table; two snakes.
                  82 × 58.
154. N 1 b (2).   'Tigris': three lizard-like creatures attacking a man who
                  defends himself with a spear. 58 × 56.
155. N 2 a (1).   'Tortuca,' tortoise (?) with a stinged tail. 'Corde'; man
                  holds a snake: three others attack his legs. 73 × 58.
156. N 2 a (2).   Three ibexes on a flat-topt rock. 45 × 51.
157. N 2 b (1).   Two cows. 78 × 63.
     N 2 b (2).   = No. 17.
158. N 3 a (1).   'Vesontis,' like a goat, climbs up a rock. 60 × 58.
159. N 3 a (2).   Two calves. 82 × 64.
160. N 3 b (1).   'Vipera' man sits at table: two snakes on it, two on floor.
                  78 × 65.

N 3 b (2). = No. 39.

N 3 b (2). = No. 48.

161. N 4 a (1). 'Uro' with a man on his horns. 85-87 × 67-64.

162. N 4 a (2). Two bears dancing. 79 × 63.

N 4 b (1). = No. 39.

N 4 b (1). = No. 48.

163. N 4 b (2). 'Uncia'; pulling down a hare which hangs on a tree. 64 × 57.

164. O 1 a (1). Fox at foot and fowl at top of tree talking. 81 × 57.

165. O 1 b (1). Unicorn placing his forefeet in a woman's lap. 82 × 62.

166. O 1 b (2). A monkey in a tree. Three others at foot. 72 × 57.

167. O 2 a (2). 'Subro.' Two hounds on its horns, one on its back, one below. 77 × 63.

O 2 b. Title-cut (No. 1) with the three figures at top cut off.

168. O 3 b. The solar system. [A.] 135 × 131.

169. O 4 a (1). Torch with broad base, two dots below. [C.] 53 × 12.

170. O 4 a (2). Long torch, line on right only. [C.] 75 × 10.

171. O 4 a (2). Fire. [C.] 38 × 22.

172. O 4 a (2). Short torch with much flame. [C.] 53 × 23.

173. O 4 a (2). Fire. [C.] 22 × 44.

O 4 b (1). = No. 173, upside down.

174. O 4 b (2). Two goats on their hind legs embracing. [C.] 41 × 23.

175. O 4 b (2). Stars falling. [C.] 50 × 24.

176. O 4 b (2). Man in flames. [C.] 45 × 23.

177. P 1 a (1). Gryphon. [C.] 24 × 50.

P 1 a (1). = No. 39.

P 1 a (1). = No. 48.

178. P 1 a (2). Eagle. 80 × 60.

179. P 2 a (1). 'Achacus,' like a duck with a hooked bill. 'Antifrigius,' with tail like a peacock. 84 × 58.

180. P 2 a (2). 'Achantis': two large and six small birds. 80 × 62.

181. P 2 b (1). Boy with three hawks, two on a perch, one on his wrist. 82 × 61.

182. P 3 a (1). 'Ariephilon,' like a large duck. 68 × 62.

183. P 3 a (2). 'Caprimulgus': one flying, one with three eggs. 82 × 63.

184. P 3 b (2). 'Alietus,' a gorgeously feathered eagle-like bird. 81 × 60.

185. P 4 a (1). 'Alcion'; swan-like bird with three young ones. 63 × 62.

186. P 4 a (2). Three small ducks swimming. 68 × 58.

187. P 4 b (1). Old man driving three geese uphill. 82 × 63.

188. Q 1 a (1). 'Ardeola': two birds facing; a smaller flies between. 37 × 62.

189. Q 1 a (1). 'Ardea.' Goose-like bird holding a large worm. 48 × 62.

190. Q 1 a (2). Two tree trunks and three bees. 54 × 66.

191. Q 1 b (2). 'Basiliscus'; bird with crown and curled scaly tail. 78 × 63.

192. Q 2 a (2). 'Barliate': two trees, with a bird on each. 67 × 58.

193. Q 2 b (2). 'Bistarda' and 'bonosa.' Small bird at top: large bird with a dead rabbit. 76 × 66.

194. Q 3 a (2). Two owls, one with a mouse. 53 × 62.

195. Q 3 b (1). 'Buteus,' etc. Three birds, one at top with long bill; another holds a fish. 82 × 62.

196. Q 3 b (2). 'Bibones.' Flies round a wine-jug, cup, and fruit. 68 × 63.

197. Q 4 a (1). 'Cantarides,' five flies. 47 × 62.

198. Q 4 b (1). 'Selintides.' Two small birds on a rock. 39 × 60.

199. Q 4 b (2). 'Caladrius.' Woman in a canopied bed looking at a crucifix. Bird perched at foot. [A.]. 89—87 × 65.

200. R 1 a (1). 'Capuijn.' Small bird on a goat's back, another sucks its udder. 54 × 57.

201. R 1 a (2). 'Carduwelis.' Bird in cage, two others perched above. 47 × 62.

202. R 1 b (1). 'Carabrion.' Small bird flying over a fire. 53 × 63.

203. R 1 b (2). 'Vliegende hert,' like a locust. 38 × 63.

204. R 1 b (2). 'Crekelen.' One on the top of something, another below. 53 × 57.

205. R 2 a (1). A stork, nest, and three young on a roof. 57 × 63.

206. R 2 b (1). Flies buzzing about a leg of mutton. 64 × 61.

207. R 2 b (2). Two trees: on one three birds, on the other one, and a nest with two young ones: two birds below. 82 × 62.

208. R 3 a (2). 'Cinomia.' Two flies, one on right with open wings. 47 × 61.

209. R 3 a (2). Dogfly. Two, one on left with open wings. 33 × 64.

210. R 3 b (1). Dove carrying a branch. [? part of set.] 56 × 63.

211. R 4 a (1). 'Coredulus,' bird picking a bone. [? part of set.] 37 × 62.

212. R 4 a (1). Bird pecking at ground at foot of a tree. 31 × 63.

213. R 4 a (1). Two tree tops: in each a raven, facing. 49 × 63.

214. R 4 a (2). 'Cocurnix.' Leafless tree: bird on branch, nest with two young ones. 43 × 63.

215. R 4 b (1). 'Cocix.' Cuckoo eating eggs in a nest: another bird above. 56 × 64.

216. R 4 b (2). Leafless tree with 3 nests (two with young) and 4 birds. 52 × 64.

217. R 4 b (2). 'Corinta,' like a guinea hen. 36 × 65.

218. S 1 a (1). 'Cocock.' Leafy tree top with bird. 54 × 62.

219. S 1 b (1). 'Cubech.' Three small birds: on the left a nest. 44 × 64.

220. S 1 b (2). Man lying under tree, attacked by flies. 38 × 62.

221. S 2 a (1). A swan. [No edge-lines: good work. A.] 56 × 53.

222. S 2 a (1). Two swans in water, one with its head under. 42 × 62.

223. S 2 a (2). 'Diomede:' three small birds perched on holed rocks(?) 39 × 62.

224. S 2 b (1). 'Draycha:' three humming birds. 32 × 57.

225. S 2 b (2). 'Echitus:' bird like quail before a hill: three flies above. 54 × 63.

226. S 3 a (1). Two falcons, one gnawing a bone, one flying up. 70 × 62.
227. S 3 b (1). = PJ. 8, with a wormhole.
      S 3 b (2). = No. 215.
228. S 4 a (1). Nightingale. Three birds on a leafless tree. 55 × 62.
229. S 4 a (1). 'Fucus.' Nine bees flying about a tree trunk. 46 × 62.
      S 4 a (2). = No. 193.
230. S 4 b (1). A cock. [Style as no. 221.] 70 × 51.
231. S 4 b (1). Two cocks fighting. 40 × 62.
232. T 1 a (1). Two pheasants. 34 × 63.
233. T 1 a (2). Eagle with a bird's head in his talons. 39 × 62.
234. T 1 a (2). Hen and four chickens. 47 × 64.
235. T 1 b (2). 'Cappuin.' Woman cutting a hen's throat: the cock looks **on.**
                  73 × 62.
      T 2 a (1). = No. 207.
236. T 2 a (2). 'Gripe.' Winged lion with a bird's beak. 80 × 62.
237. T 2 b (1). = PJ. 3.
238. T 2 b (2). 'Gricocenderon;' like a swan. 61 × 63.
239. T 2 b (2). 'Girfalco,' bites another bird's neck. Small **bird on** top of hill
                  above; nest halfway down. 77 × 64.
240. T 3 a (1). = PJ. 4.
241. T 3 b (1). Five cranes flying to the left. 29 × 62.
242. T 3 b (1). A church with two towers. Birds flying **about it.** **61 × 63.**
243. T 3 b (2). Harpy standing on a prostrate man. 80 **× 63.**
      T 4 a (1). = No. 242.
244. T 4 a (2). Dog and bird fighting for a running rabbit. 55 × 62.
245. T 4 b (1). Ibis holding fish : two fish in river. 53 × 64.
246. T 4 b (2). 'Ibos :' two long-necked birds and a horse. 76 × 62.
247. V 1 a (1). Cistern at foot of cliff : three birds on the edge. 76 × 64.
248. V 1 a (2). 'Kiches.' Two leafless trees : on one 3 birds, on the other a
                  nest and a bird flying to it. 55 × 62.
249. V 1 b (1). 'Kinnius ;' birds on and about a stone. **37 × 63.**
250. V 1 b (2). 'Lagus.' Bird with eel swimming to tree on which **is a** nest
                  with 7 young. 79 × 62.
251. V 1 b (2). 'Laagepus.' Bird with rabbit's head. 47 × 64.
252. V 2 a (1). 'Lymachus.' Leafless tree-top with nest ; in it a bird and two
                  young. 43 × 63.
      V 2 a (2). = No. 228.
253. V **2 b** (1). 'Magnales,' like a heron, with a fish in its mouth. 84 × 62.
254. V 2 b (1). 'Meerle.' One in cage, one on tree-trunk, conversing.
                  53 × 63.
      V 2 b (2). = No. 182.
255. V 3 a (1). 'Meropus,' ties its neck in a knot. Smaller bird in front with
                  prey. 74 × 62.
      V 3 a (2). = No. 250.

V 3 b (2).   = No. 219.
V 3 b (2).   = No. 186.
V 4 a (1).   = No. 212.
V 4 a (1).   = No. 234.
V 4 b (1).   = No. 211.
V 4 b (2).   = No. 181.
256. X 1 a (1).   **Magpie** holding a coin. Above, small bird surrounded by six flies. 84 × 58.
X 1 a (2).   = No. 196.
257. x 1 b (2).   'Opimachus,' like a rabbit with wings and beak. 67 × 62.
258. x 2 a (1).   'Nepas.' Long-billed bird picking up worms. 46 × 60.
259. x 2 a (2).   'Onocraculus,' like a swan pecking at objects on the ground. 61 × 60.
260. x 2 b (1).   'Osyna,' etc. One bird swimming, another flying, holding a large bone. 80 × 62.
x 2 b (2).   = No. 194.
261. x 3 a (1).   Old woman with a stick, a basket on her head, **walking.** 79 × 62.
262. x 3 b (1).   'Passer.' Four birds in a cornfield. 62 × 65.
263. x 4 a (1).   Two peacocks, one with tail displayed. 81 × 62.
x 4 b (1).   = No. 213.
x 4 b (1).   = No. 212.
264. x 4 b (2).   At back a bird swimming; one in front guzzling frogs. 61 × 62.
Y 1 a (1).   = No. 241, upside down.
265. Y 1 a (1).   Leafless tree top. On extreme left a nest: bird perched near it. 39-7 × 61.
Y 1 a (2).   = No. 207.
Y 1 b (1).   = No. 264.
266. Y 1 b (2).   'Butterflies.' Five flies round a flower. 51 × 61.
267. Y 2 a (1).   The pelican in her piety: 3 young ones. 82 × 69.
Y 2 b (1).   = No. 180.
268. Y 3 a (1).   'Exter.' Two rook-like birds on roofs, conversing. 57 × 62.
Y 3 a (2).   = No. 252.
269. Y 3 b (1).   'Papegaye,' with a collar round its neck. 60 × **66.**
270. Y 3 b (2).   Five flies around flames issuing from a furnace. **84 × 62.**
Y 4 a (1).   = No. 238.
Y 4 a (2).   = No. 216.
Y 4 b (1).   = No. 139.
Y 4 b (2).   = No. 225.
Aa 1 a (1).   = No. 220.
271. Aa 1 a (2).   'Strix:' bird in water feeds 2 young: two different birds above. **54 × 58.**
Aa 1 b (1).   = No. 189.

272. **Aa 1 b** (2). Sort of winged mule: above small birds on a truss of hay. 88 × 62.

273. Aa 2 a (2). 'Tarda,' etc. Two birds, the upper has curly horns. **83 × 62.**

274. Aa 2 b (1). Two birds on a tree conversing. 52 **×** 62.

275. Aa 3 a (1). Man climbing a tree to a nest. 78 × 54.

Aa 3 a (2). = No. 229.

276. Aa 3 b (1). Three owls in a leafy tree-top. 60 × **61.**

277. Aa 3 b (2). Hoopoe, large crested bird. 73 × 63.

278. Aa 4 a (2). Bird with webbed feet pecks at a grassy hillock. Two similar birds above. 54 × 63.

279. Aa 4 a (2). 'Vleermuys.' 5 bats (?) fly to one seated on a rock. 58 × **67.**

280. Aa 4 b. = FT. 7.

Bb 1 a. ■ No. 1, with the top part cut off as before.

281 Bb 2 a (1). Numerous fish in the water below a boat. 72 × 64.

282. Bb 2 a (2). Man putting an eel into a basket. 73 × 60.

283. Bb 2 b (1). Man packing herring in a barrel. 79 × 58.

284. Bb 2 b (2). Three crowned fish on a shield. [A.]

285. Bb 3 a (1). 1 large, 3 small, and 1 large fish, the last in a net. 74 × 64.

286. Bb 3 a (2). Large fish with fire and a vessel on his back. Below, another fish. 77 × 67.

Bb 3 b (1). = No. 138.

287. Bb 3 b (1). Several small fish below a willow. 73 × 66.

288. Bb 3 b (2). ' Aureū vellus.' Three small round fish. 41 × 66.

289. Bb 4 a (1). Two large and one small fish swimming round the **foot of** a cliff. 51 × 62.

290. Bb 4 a (2). 'Abydes.' Fish with four legs and animal's head. 59 × 58.

291. Bb 4 a (2). Two flat fish, 'Ahune,' with ears and pigs' tails. 58 × 58.

292. Bb 4 b (2). Two large fish swimming to a net in which are six small fish. 69 × 61.

293. **Bb 4** b (2). Two eels, two flat fish, and a large fish with another in its mouth. 74 × 63.

294. Cc 1 a (1). A merman. 72 × 57.

295. Cc 1 a (2). A large fish, and 3 smaller ones. The lowest touches the bottom of the cut. 70 × 60.

296. Cc 1 b (1). Lobster with six legs and two claws. 76 × 57.

297. Cc 2 a (1). Two dogs with scales and fins. 87 × 65.

298. Cc 2 a (2). Three fish, the middle one horned. The lowest caught by a man seated on the shore. 77 × 65.

299. Cc 2 b (1). 'Cetus,' the whale. Sideways. 67 × 83.

300. Cc 3 a (1). Lobster with eight legs and two claws. 54 × 67.

301. Cc 3 a (1). Otter-like animal with fish's tail. 27 × 64.

302. Cc 3 a (2). Small oval beast with two legs, and a quadruped with a man's head, fins, and scales. 77 × 57.

303. Cc 3 b (1). 'Mussels,' like whelks. 36 × 58.

304. Cc 3 b (2).   Four 'Cockles,' similar.   48 × 57.
305. Cc 3 b (2).   Fish with bird's head; conger eel.   50 × 56.
306. Cc 4 a (1).   'Cocodrillus,' like a bear.   Two birds fly towards his mouth.   60 × 58.
307 Cc 4 b (1).   Sea dragon, upside down.   74 × 65.
308. Cc 4 b (2).   Two mermaids without faces.   'Dolphins.'   68 × 55.
309. Dd 1 a (1).   A fish: below, a shell fish with pig's head, upside down.   [*Block split.*]   60 × 61.
310. Dd 1 a (2).   Three fish: one bristly, one long, one flat.   87 × 66.
311. Dd 1 b (1).   Small animal with two young: cow: cow-like animal with fish's tail.   82 × 63.
312. Dd 1 b (2).   Two long fish; cut sideways.   53 × 73.
313. Dd 2 a (1).   Three animals with fish's tails (like a cow, sheep, and calf).   85 × 64.
314. Dd 2 a (2).   A large fish lying on the sea-bottom: above its tail, a group of fish like sprats.   48 × 63.
315. Dd 2 b (1).   'Estinis,' a cray fish; eight legs.   47 × 69.
316. Dd 2 b (2).   'Erox:' two large fish, one with turned-down, one with turned-up nose.   55 × 59.
317. Dd 3 a (1).   A ship: six fish sticking to her bottom: others on rocks, etc.   79 × 58.
318. Dd 3 a (2).   'Esox;' two large fish, the upper facing right, the lower left.   Sideways.   63 × 82.
     Dd 3 b (1).   = No. 311.
319. Dd 3 b (2).   Three fish: the middle one has six small ones around his mouth.   76 × 57.
320 Dd 4 a (1).   Fish with eight black legs: below, three small fish.   45 × 57.
321. Dd 4 a (2).   'Gobio,' a flat fish: below, two small ones on a rounded rock.   58 × 54.
322. Dd 4 b (1).   Fish with duck's feet: animal like beaver on a spit of land.   74 × 65.
323. Dd 4 b (2).   Four flying (?) fish, and another fish below.   Sideways.   56 × 72.
324. Dd 4 b (2).   'Icinus marinus,' a hedgehog, apparently standing in shallow water.   34 × 68.
325. Ee 1 a (1).   Three fish: the upper has a curly shell, the middle one a hump.   75 × 63.
326. Ee 1 a (2).   'Karabo,' a large fish facing right: below, an eel.   58 × 68.
327. Ee 1 b (1).   'Koky.'   Beast with cow's head, scaly body, and four hands.   73 × 66.
328. Ee 1 b (2).   Sea lion.   86 × 64.
329. Ee 1 b (2).   Two sea hares.   62 × 58.
330. Ee 2 a (1).   Sea serpent with three wings, and small winged dragon-like quadruped.   87 × 65.

331. Ee 2 a (2). 'Loligo.' Large fish curled in crescent shape. **Sideways.** 57 × 69.

332. Ee 2 b (1). Sea locust (two legs only). 35 × 61.

333. Ee 2 b (2). Two small fishes between two large ones. 76 × 63.

334. Ee 3 a (1). Two sea wolves. 75 × 65.

335. Ee 3 a (2). Bird with crest and fish tail: below, fish with head like a **fox.** 77 × 59.

336. Ee 3 b (1). Man catching fish with a shrimp net. 85 × 64.

337. Ee 3 b (2). Two sea mice: two sea snails: two other small animals. 73 × 62.

338. Ee 4 a (1). 'Murex,' with a stick in its mouth. 47 × 57.
　　　Ee 4 a (2). = No. 60.

339. Ee **4** b (1). 'Multipes.' Six-legged locust. Below, egg surrounded **by** sticks. 73 × 58.

340. Ee 4 b (2). Four fish at the foot of a cliff. 64 × 58.

341. Ff 1 a (1). Sea monk and sea unicorn. 83 × 58.

342. Ff 1 a (2). A net held by two men: below, a sea horse, etc. 72 × 58.

343. Ff 1 b (1). 'Nereydes:' a merman and a sea monkey. 86 × 62.

344. Ff 1 b (2). 'Orbis;' large round fish. 43 × 58.

345. Ff 1 b (2). 'Oysters;' like snails, each with several heads. 45 × 58.
　　　Ff 2 a (1). = No. 335.

346. Ff 2 a (2). Mermaid holding her tail. Below, an oval shell-fish. 81-79 × 63.

347. Ff 2 b (1). 'Pistris' climbing over a ship. 72 × 58.

348. Ff 2 b (1). A pig running at a fish: below, three round stones. 43 × 68.

349. Ff 2 b (2). Boar with fins and fish's tail. Sideways. 61 × 80.

350. Ff 3 a (1). 'Polypus:' scaly creature with eight legs. 37 × 57.

351. Ff 3 a (2). Two spotted fish. Sideways. 38 × 72.

352. Ff 3 b (1). Three large molluscs: below, four small fish. 62 × 60.

353. Ff 3 b (2). Long fish with twisted tail and half-human face. Two spotted flat fish. 53 × 55.
　　　Ff 3 b (2). = No. 131.
　　　Ff 4 a (1). = No. 30.

354. Ff 4 a (1). Two fish curled in a circle; below, long fish with a human face in its belly. 65 × 57.

355. Ff 4 a (2). 'Salmon,' etc.; three fish, the upper two close together, the third with a very curious head. 77 × 64.

356. Ff 4 b (1). Three fish: the top one hideous: the middle one in a net, the lower edge of which is lifted by the third. 84 × 62.

357. Ff 4 b (2). Three very ugly fish. 34 × 70.

358. Gg 1 a (1). A ship: close under it a fish: below, a merman. 79 × 57.

359. Gg 1 a (2). Siren; a mermaid with two tails, which she holds. 50 × 67.

360. Gg 1 b (1). Two fish, the upper very prickly. Sideways. 57 × 68.

361. Gg 1 b (2). The sun shining on four fish. 48 × 58.

362. Gg 2 a (1). A wriggly creature with ten legs, and a small quadruped with long tail ending in a sting. 58 × 53.

363. Gg 2 a (2). Two long and two round fish to the right of rocks. 47 × 61.

364. Gg 2 b (1). 'Stoncus,' a sort of lizard, with spots. 41 × 61.

365. Gg 2 b (2). 'Sturio,' a large fish above two rocks. 37 × 57.

366. Gg 3 a (1). Four 'starfish,' all jags. 42 × 60.

367. Gg 3 a (2). Apparently meant for three fish with their snouts against rocks on the right. 43 × 60.

368. Gg 3 a (2). A white eel and two other fish in a descending scale as to size. Sideways. 52 × 66.

369. Gg 3 b (1). Fish in a nest **at top of tree**; another climbs trunk: third fish **at bottom.** 82 × 62.

Gg 3 b (2). = **No. 332.**

Gg 4 a (1). = No. 352.

370. Gg 4 a (2). 'Tigruis,' like a poodle: two spotted fish below. 73 × 62.

371 Gg 4 b (1). 'Tinnus,' prickly beast climbing into a ship. 81 × 61.

372. Gg 4 b (1). 'Tortuca,' like a pig with a drum for body. **57 × 57.**

373. Gg 4 b (2). Shaggy sea cow and calf. 72 × 63.

374. Hh 1 a (1). Serpent with a large curved horn and **twisted** tail: a large spotted flat fish below. 53 × 60.

375. Hh 1 a (2). Three fish between broken edges of ice (?). 52 × 66.

376. Hh 1 b (1). Three creatures : the middle one a fish with two heads and three tails : the lower like a scaly dog. 84 × 57.

377. Hh 1 b (2). 'Ypotamus;' beaked horse, pecking at its own back. 58 × 60.

378. Hh 2 a (2). 'Zedrosus,' etc. Three remarkable creatures : the middle one smooth, the rest shaggy. 84 × 62.

379. Hh 2 b (1). The upper half is a man in armour : the lower a scaly fish's tail.

Hh 2 b (2). The middle figure from the top of the title cut, No. 1.

380. Hh 3 a (1). Creature with owl's face and hedgehog's body. 33 × 58.

Hh 3 a (1). = No. 340.

381. Hh 3 a. = FT. 5.

Hh 3 a. The two side figures from the top of No. 1, placed sideways on each side of No. 382.

382. Hh 4 b. Device.

22. The New Lands.

The cuts in this book are for the most part a collection of those in the three books, Nos. 2, 3, 4; one comes from No. 1. No. 19 occurs in the Chronicle of 1530. No. 18 seems to be by the same hand as the *Oesrpronck* set C. No. 1 is interesting, as apparently belonging (with DP. 126) to a lost book like PJ., NW., and RL.

1. Fo. 1 a. Male and female savage with 2 children. A bleeding head hangs on a tree (same style as those in NW. and RL.). 66 × 63.

2. 1 b.   = PJ. 2.
3. 1 b.   = PJ. 3.
4. 1 b.   = PJ. 8.
5. 1 b.   = PJ. 5.
   2 a.   = No. 1.
6. 3 a.   = RL. 1.
7. 3 b.   = RL. 2.
8. 4 b.   = RL. 3.
9. 5 a.   Siege of a fortified gate with portcullis. Scaling ladder.   120 × 89.
10. 5 b.   = RL. 4.
11. 6 b.   = RL. 6.
12. 7 b.   = RL. 5.
13. 8 a.   = NW. 1.
14. 8 b, 9 a.   = RL. 7.
15. 9 b.   Two angels show the host to a kneeling worshipper : around is a rosary. 66 × 67.
16. 10 a.   = FT. 25.
17. 10 a.   The Virgin, a sword piercing her neck.   63 × 37.
18. 11 a.   Thomas puts his hand into Christ's side.   [Cf. O. 166.]   56 × 47.
19. 12 b.   A body of knights riding. One horse has thrown its rider. [Injured.] 91 × 69.
   16 a.   = No. 2.
   16 b.   = No. 5.
20. 17 a.   = PJ. 6.
21. 18 a.   = PJ. 4.
22. 18 b.   = PJ. 7.
   19 a.   = No. 4.
   20 a.   = No. 3.
23. 21 b.   = PJ. 1.
24. 22 a.   = PJ. 9.
25. 24 a.   = V. 15.
26. 24 b.   Device 3 в.

23. The wonderful shape.

The cuts are almost all the same as in the *Ditren Palleys*, the smaller number being due partly to omissions, partly to the imperfection of the only copy. There are, however, a few cuts which are new : nearly all (Nos. 33, 49, 53, etc.) belong to the ordinary set. The reader is, however, warned that owing to the large number of cuts, and the impossibility of examining the actual books side by side, the identification, or the contrary, of particular cuts is in a few cases uncertain, though it is hoped that no serious mistake has been made. The only new cut not belonging to the set is No. 326, one of the grammar-cuts of a master and pupils which are so common at this period.

71

1. a 2 a (2). = DP. 4, O. 13.
2. a 3 a (1). = V. 9.
   a 3 a (2). = No. 1.
3. a 3 b, 4 a. = DP. 5.
4. a 3 b, 4 a. = DP. 6.
5. a 4 b. = DP. 7, the heart not inked in.
6. a 5 a. = DP. 8.
7-12. a 5 b. = DP. 9-14.
13. b 1 a (2). = DP. 16.
14. b 1 b (1). = DP. 17.
15. b 4 a (1). = DP. 23, V. 14.
16. b 4 a (2). = DP. 24.
17. b 4 b (1). = DP. 25.
18. b 4 b (2). = DP. 26.
19. c 1 a (1). = DP. 34.
20. c 1 a (2). = DP. 28.
21. c 1 b (2). = DP. 29.
22. c 2 a (1). = DP. 30.
23. c 2 a (2). = DP. 31.
24. c 2 b (2). = DP. 32.
25. c 3 a (1). = DP. 167.
   c 3 a (2). = No. 19.
26. c 3 a (2). = DP. 35.
27. c 3 b (1). = DP. 36.
28. c 3 b (2). = DP. 38.
29. c 4 a (1). = DP. 40.
30. c 4 b (1). = DP. 41.
31. c 4 b (2). = DP. 42.
32. d 1 a (2). = DP. 43.
33. d 1 b (1). Cameleopard [not DP. 44?]. 80×62.
34. d 1 b (2). = DP. 46.
35. d 2 a (1). = DP. 47.
36. d 2 b (1). = DP. 49.
37. d 2 b (1). 'Calopus.' = DP. 63.
38. d 2 b (2). = DP. 51.
39. d 3 a (2). = DP. 52.
40. d 3 b (1). = DP. 53.
41. d 3 b (1). = DP. 54.
42. d 3 b (2). = DP. 55.
43. d 4 a (1). = DP. 56
44. d 4 a (1). 'Cicade.' = DP. 57.
45. d 4 a (2). = DP. 58.

46. d 4 a (2). = DP. 59.
47. d 4 b (1). Adders. = DP. 60.
48. d 4 b (2). = DP. 61.
49. e 1 a (1). Man facing tree; the illustration to 'coney.' 60×62.
50. e 1 a (2). 'Damma.' = DP. 50.
51. e 1 a (2). = DP. 64.
52. e 1 b (1). = DP. 65.
53. e 2 a (1). 'Gray;' like a hairy pig. 43×57.
54. e 2 a (1). = DP. 67.
55. e 2 a (2). = DP. 69.
56. e 2 b (1). = DP. 70.
57. e 2 b (1). = DP. 71.
58. e 2 b (2). = DP. 72.
59. e 3 a (1). = DP. 73.
60. e 3 b (2). = DP. 74.
61. e 4 a (1). = DP. 75.
62. e 4 a (2). = DP. 76.
63. e 4 b (1). = DP. 77.
64. e 4 b (1). = DP. 78.
65. e 4 b (2). = DP. 79.
66. e 4 b (2). = DP. 80: broken, only 67×63.
67. f 1 a (1). = DP. 81.
68. f 1 a (2). = DP. 82.
69. f 1 b (1). = DP. 83.
70. f 1 b (2). = DP. 85.
71. f 2 a (1). = DP. 84.
72. f 2 a (2). = DP. 86.
73. f 2 a (2). = DP. 87.
74. f 2 b (1). = DP. 88.
75. f 2 b (2). = DP. 89.
   f 2 b (2). 'Histrix.' = No. 53.
76. f 3 a (1). = DP. 91.
77. f 3 a (2). = DP. 92.
78. f 3 b (1). = DP. 93.
79. f 3 b (1). = DP. 94.
80. f 3 b (2). = DP. 95.
81. f 3 b (2). = DP. 96.
   g 1 a (1). 'Leviathan.' = No. 52.
82. g 1 a (2). = DP. 101.

g 1 b (1). 'Lintworme.' = No. 45.

83. g 1 b (2). = DP. 33 ; broken, only 57 × 67.

84. g 1 b (2). = DP. 102.

85. g 2 a (1). = DP. 103.

86. g 2 a (2). = DP. 104.

87. g 2 a (2). = DP. 105.

88. g 2 b (1). = DP. 106.

89. g 2 b (1). = DP. 107.

90. g 2 b (2). = DP. 108.

91. g 3 a (1). = DP. 109.

92. g 3 a (2). = DP. 110.

93. g 3 a (2). = DP. 111.

94. g 3 b (1). = DP. 19.

95. g 3 b (2). = DP. 112.

96. g 4 a (1). = DP. 113.

97. g 4 a (2). = DP. 137.

98. g 4 b (1). = DP. 114.

99. g 4 b (1). = DP. 115, upside down.

100. g 4 b (1). = DP. 116.

101. g 4 b (2). = DP. 117.

102. h 1 a (1). = DP. 118.
h 1 a (2). = No. 76.

103. h 1 b (1). = DP. 119.
h 1 b (1). = No. 84.

104. h 1 b (2). = DP. 120.

105. h 2 a (1). = DP. 121.

106. h 2 a (1). = DP. 122.

107. h 2 a (2). = PJ. 1.

108. h 2 b (1). = DP. 124.

109. h 2 b (1). = DP. 124.

110. h 2 b (2). = DP. 127.

111. h 2 b (2). = DP. 126.

112. h 3 a (1). = DP. 128.

113. h 3 a (2). = DP. 152.

114. h 3 a (2). = DP. 129.

115. h 3 b (1). = DP. 130.

116. h 3 b (2). = DP.131, sideways.

117. h 4 a (1). = DP. 132.

118. h 4 a (2). = DP. 133.
h 4 a (2). = No. 95.

119. h 4 b (1). = DP. 151.

120. h 4 b (2). = DP. 134.

121. i 1 a (1). = DP. 135

122. i 1 a (1). = DP. 136.

123. i 1 a (2). = DP. 140.

124. i 1 b (1). = DP. 142.

125. i 1 b (1). = DP. 141.

126. i 1 b (2). = DP. 143.

127. i 2 a (1). = DP. 144.

128. i 2 a (2). = DP. 145.
i 2 a (2). = No. 36.

129. i 2 b (1). 'Tarandus.' Hairy, with deer's head and long curly horns. One paw raised. 80 × 64. [Cf. DP. 44.]

130. i 2 b (2). = DP. 147.

131. i 3 a (1). = DP. 148.

132. i 3 a (1). = DP. 149.

133. i 3 a (2). = DP. 150.

134. i 3 b (1). = DP. 153.

135. i 3 b (2). = DP. 154.

136. i 3 b (2). = DP. 155.

137. i 4 a (1). = DP. 160.

138. i 4 a (2). = DP. 161.

139. i 4 b (1). = DP. 162.

140. i 4 b (2). = DP. 163.

141. i 4 b (2). = DP. 164.

142. k 1 a (1). = DP. 165.

143. k 1 a (2). = DP. 166.

144. k 1 b. = FT. 7.
k 2 a (2). = No. 5.

145. k 2 b. = DP. 168.

146. k 3 a (2). = DP. 178.

147. k 3 b (2). = DP. 179.

148. k 4 a (1). = DP. 180.

149. k 4 a (2). = DP. 181.

150. k 4 b (1). = DP. 182.

151. k 4 b (2). = DP. 183.

152. l 1 a (1). = DP. 184.

153. l 1 a (2). = DP. 185.

154. l 1 b (1). = DP. 186.

155. l 1 b (2). = DP. 187.

156. l 2 a (1). = DP. 188.

157. l 2 a (2). = DP. 190.

158. l 2 a (2). = DP. 191.

L

159. l 2 b (2).   = DP. 192.
160. l 2 b (2).   = DP. 193.
161. l 3 a (1).   = DP. 194.
162. l 3 a (2).   = DP. 195.
163. l 3 b (1).   = DP. 196.
164. l 3 b (1).   = DP. 197.
165. l 3 b (2).   = DP. 198.
166. l 4 a (1).   = DP. 199.
167. l 4 a (2).   = DP. 200.
168. l 4 a (2).   = DP. 201.
169. l 4 b (1).   = DP. 202.
170. l 4 b (1).   = DP. 203.
171. l 4 b (2).   = DP. 204.
172. l 4 b (2).   = DP. 205.
173. m 1 a (2).   = DP. 221
174. m 1 a (2).   = DP. 222.
175. m 1 b (1).   = DP. 207.
176. m 1 b (2).   = DP. 209.
177. m 1 b (2).   = DP. 206.
178. m 2 a (1).   = DP. 210.
179. m 2 a (2).   = DP. 211
180. m 2 a (2).   = DP. 212.
181. m 2 b (1).   = DP. 213.
182. m 2 b (1).   = DP. 214.
183. m 2 b (2).   = DP. 215.
184. m 2 b (2).   = DP. 216.
185. m 3 a (1).   = DP. 217.
186. m 3 a (1).   = DP. 218.
187 m 3 a (2).   = DP. 219.
188. m 3 b (1).   = DP. 220.
189. m 3 b (1).   = DP. 223.
190. m 3 b (2).   = DP. 224.
191. m 3 b (2).   = DP. 225.
192. m 4 a (1).   = DP. 226.
193. m 4 a (2).   = DP. 232.
     m 4 b (1).   = No. 187.
194. m 4 b (2).   = PJ. 8.
195. n 1 a (1).   = DP. 228.
     n 1 a (1).   = No. 160.
196. n 1 a (2).   = DP. 229.
197. n 1 b (1).   = DP. 231.
198. n 1 b (1).   = DP. 234.
199. n 1 b (2).   = DP. 235.
     n 2 a (1).   = No. 175.

200. n 2 a (2).   = DP. 236.
201. n 2 b (1).   = DP. 238.
202. n 2 b (2).   = PJ. 4.
203. n 3 a (1).   = DP. 241.
204. n 3 a (1).   = DP. 242.
205. n 3 a (2).   = DP. 243.
     n 3 b (1).   = No. 204.
206. n 3 b (1).   = DP. 244.
207. n 3 b (2).   = DP. 245.
208. n 4 a (1).   = DP. 246.
209. n 4 a (1).   = DP. 247.
210. n 4 a (2).   = DP. 248.
211. n 4 b (1).   = DP. 249.
212. n 4 b (1).   At top a round ob-
     ject. In front, a duck swim-
     ming, holding a fish. 35 × 59.
213. n 4 b (2).   = DP. 251.
214. n 4 b (2).   = DP. 252.
215. o 1 a (1).   = DP. 253.
216. o 1 a (1).   = DP. 254.
     o 1 a (2).   = No. 150.
217. o 1 a (2).   = DP. 255.
218. o 1 b (1).   = DP. 250.
     o 1 b (2).   = No. 154.
219. o 2 a (1).   = DP. 233.
220. o 2 a (1).   = DP. 256.
     o 2 a (2).   = No. 163.
     o 2 b (1).   = No. 179.
     o 2 b (1).   = No. 149.
     o 2 b (2).   = No. 175.
221. o 3 a (1).   = DP. 258.
222. o 3 a (2).   = DP. 257.
223. o 3 a (2).   = DP. 260.
     o 3 b (1).   = No. 161.
224. o 3 b (2).   = DP. 261.
225. o 4 a (1).   = DP. 262.
226. o 4 a (2).   = DP. 263.
     o 4 b (1).   = No. 181.
     o 4 b (1).   = No. 180.
227. o 4 b (2).   = DP. 264.
228. o 4 b (2).   Black ground. Cloud
     pattern and white rain. Below,
     nine 'butterflies' and parts of
     two others. 60 × 50.

229. p 1 a (1). = DP. 267.
    p 1 b (1). = No. 148.
230. p 1 b (2). = DP. 268.
    p 1 b (2). = No. 214.
231. p 2 a (1). = DP. 270.
232. p 2 a (2). = DP. 269.
    p 2 a (2). = No. 201.
    p 2 b (1). = No. 184.
233. p 2 b (2). = DP. 139.
    p 2 b (2). = No. 191.
    p 3 a (1). = No. 188.
234. p 3 a (1). = DP. 271.
235. p 3 a (2). = DP. 189.
236. p 3 b (1). = DP. 272.
237. p 3 b (2). = DP. 273.
238. p 3 b (2). Bird in air, with a sort of ring below its tail. Below, a nest with two small birds floating on waves. 77 × 68.
239. p 4 a (1). ■ DP. 274.
240. p 4 a (2). ■ DP. 275.
241. p 4 a (2). ■ DP. 279, sideways.
242. p 4 b (1). ■ DP. 266. Here 'wasps.'
243. p 4 b (2). = DP. 276.
244. q 1 a (1). ■ DP. 277.
245. q 1 a. ■ DP. 37.
246. q 1 a. = DP. 48.
247. q 1 a. = FT. 5.
248. q 1 b (1). = DP. 281.
249. q 1 b (2). = DP. 282.
250. q 1 b (2). = DP. 284.
251. q 2 a (1). = DP. 283.
252. q 2 a (1). = DP. 285.
253. q 2 a (2). = DP. 286.
254. q 2 b (1). ■ DP. 287.
255. q 2 b (2). = DP. 288.
256. q 2 b (2). = DP. 289.
257. q 3 a (1). = DP. 290.
258. q 3 a (1). = DP. 291.
259. q 3 a (2). = DP. 292.
260. q 3 b (1). = DP. 293.
261. q 3 b (2). = DP. 294.
262. q 3 b (2). = DP. 295.

263. q 4 a (1). = DP. 296.
264. q 4 a (2). = DP. 297.
265. q 4 b (1). = DP. 298.
266. q 4 b (2). = DP. 299.
267. r 1 a (1). ■ DP. 300.
268. r 1 a (1). ■ DP. 301.
269. r 1 a (2). ■ DP. 302.
270. r 1 b (1). ■ DP. 303.
271. r 1 b (1). = DP. 304.
272. r 1 b (2). ■ DP. 305.
273. r 2 a (1). ■ DP. 306.
274. r 2 a (1). = DP. 307.
275. r 2 a (2). = DP. 308.
276. r 2 b (1). = DP. 309.
277. r 2 b (2). = DP. 311.
278. r 3 a (1). ■ DP. 312, sideways.
279. r 3 a (2). = DP. 313.
280. r 3 b (1). = DP. 314.
281. r 3 b (1). = DP. 315.
282. r 3 b (1). ■ DP. 316.
283. r 3 b (2). = DP. 317.
284. r 4 a (1). ■ DP. 318.
    r 4 a (2). ■ No. 277.
285. r 4 b (1). = DP. 319.
286. r 4 b (1). = DP. 320.
287. r 4 b (2). = DP. 321.
288. s 1 a (1). = DP. 322.
289. s 1 a (1). = DP. 323, straight.
290. s 1 a (2). = DP. 324.
291. s 1 a (2). = DP. 325.
292. s 1 b (1). = DP. 326.
293. s 1 b (2). = DP. 327.
294. s 1 b (2). = DP. 328.
295. s 2 a (1). = DP. 330.
    s 2 a (2). = No. 48.
296. s 2 b (1). = DP. 332.
297. s 2 b (1). = DP. 333.
298. s 2 b (2). Two sea-wolves: a different cut from DP. 334. 80 × 57.
299. s 3 a (1). ■ DP. 335.
300. s 3 a (2). ■ DP. 336.
301. s 3 a (2). ■ DP. 337.
302. s 3 b (1). ■ DP. 338.

s 3 b (2). = No. 47.	320. t 3 a (2). = DP. 357.
303. s 3 b (2). = DP. 339.	321. t 3 a (2). = DP. 358.
304. s 4 a (1). = DP. 340, upside down.	322. t 3 b (1). = DP. 359.
	323. t 3 b (2). = DP. 360, straight.
305. s 4 a (2). = DP. 341.	324. t 4 a (1). = DP. 361.
306. s 4 b (1). = DP. 342.	t 4 a (1). = No. 317.
307. s 4 b (1). = DP. 343.	325. t 4 b (1). = DP. 365, upside down.
308. s 4 b (2). = DP. 344.	
309. s 4 b (2). = DP. 345.	326. t 4 b (2). = DP. 366.
t 1 a (1). = No. 299.	327. t 4 b (2). = DP. 367.
310. t 1 a (2). = DP. 346.	328. v 3 a (1). = DP. 379.
311. t 1 a (2). = DP. 347.	329. v 3 a (2). A man teaching with his fingers, a book on his lap. The bottom of the cut projects outwards like a sort of handle. 82 × 47
312. t 1 b (1). = DP. 349.	
313. t 1 b (2). = DP. 350.	
314. t 1 b (2). = DP. 351.	
315. t 2 a (1). = DP. 352.	
316. t 2 a (1). = DP. 353.	330. v 3 a (2). = DP. 380.
t 2 a (2). = No. 116.	331. v 3 b (1). = MN. 5.
t 2 b (1). = No. 22.	332. v 3 b (2). The two sides of the top part of DP. 1.
317. t 2 b (1). = DP. 354.	v 3 b (2). = No. 245.
318. t 2 b (2). = DP. 355.	v 3 b (2). = No. 246.
319. t 3 a (1). = DP. 356.	

24. Van Jason ende Hercules.

There are, according to the *Bibliophile Belge*, 37 cuts in this book, four of which are on the title.

25. Die historie van Hercules.

The cuts in this book are repeated from those in No. 24. Two cuts and a border are on the title-page, and there is one cut after the colophon.

26. The parson of Kalenborowe.

These cuts, which are all of one set, are of a most excruciating character; the woodcutter has not the slightest notion of either design or execution.

1. 5 b. Two peasants drinking under a tree. 63 × 43.
2. 5 b. The parson with wings on battlements: below, a cask. 63 × 33.
3. 7 a. The parson at mass. 66 × 47
4. 10 a. The parson and bishop at the foot of some steps. 66 × 46.
5. 11 a. The parson talks with the bishop's lady. 69 × 64.
6. 12 a. The parson under the bishop's bed. 66 × 67.
7. 13 a. The parson washing. 38 × 35.
8. 13 a. The duchess and her gentleman riding by. 53 × 73.

9. 16 a. The parson brings two peasants naked before the duke. 64 × 83.

10. 19 b. The parson shews the duke his horse on a trencher. 66 × 72.

11. 21 a. The parson on his horse in a dung cart. 57 × 87.

12. 22 a. = FJ. 3.

13. 23 b. The parson's breeches borne as a banner. 61 **× 37.**

14. 23 b. Two peasants following the same. 60 × 37.

15. 24 a. **Two** cows. 62 × 26.

16. 24 a. The parson in his vestments in a field. 62 × 33.

     25 a. = No. 16.

17. 25 a. Bailiff and churchwarden. 66 × 39.

27. Der IX quaesten.

According to the *Bibliophile Belge*, there are 35 cuts, many of peculiar style, in this work, including:

1. On title, repeated in the work ; Mohammed and Mary surprised in bed together by Mohammed's wife Cadiga.

2. Fo. 20 b. A man in monkish costume, brandishing in his left hand a huge sword, preaches in a church to a group of nuns.

3. The joys of the Mohammedan paradise.

4. A cut between two borders, of Mohammed carried by three devils into hell.

5. Judas killing his father ; a beautiful landscape.

6. Device 3 B.

28. Tdal sonder wederkeeren.

The following description of the illustrations in this book is taken from Vanderhaeghen and the reprint mentioned in Part II.

1. **Fo.** 1 a. Death holding an arrow, seated on a coffin in a tent, which occupies a narrow pass between rocks. The pass on each side of the tent is blocked with corpses. On the rocks on the left is 'Accident' seated on a tusked animal which has crossbows for ears, daggers for a mane ; two of its legs are swords, and two birch rods ; its tail is formed by a three-headed snake. On the rocks on the right is 'Antike,' an old man on crutches, and 'Maladie,' a woman seated. (In facsimile 123 × 119 mm.) Reproduced in the reprint.

2. 3 b. 'Accident' from the title cut.

3. 3 b. Side-piece, 'Actor.'

4. 5 b. 'Antike' and 'Maladie' from the title cut.

5. 5 b. Side-piece, Death carrying a coffin.

6. 7 b. 'Oudtheyt.'

   7 b. = No. 5.

7. 9 b. 'Exces' as death's herald.

8. 9 b. Persons of different conditions at his side.

9. **12 a.** Death drags to him an emperor, a king of France, and a prince.

10. **12 b.** Death attacking burghers.

11. 14 a. Man reading; a vignette [probably = BC. 119].
12. 15 b. 'Lustige jeuchden,' two naked women.
    15 b. = No. 6.
13. 16 b. Device 3 B.

29. Brabant Chronicle, 1530.

The chief set of cuts used in this book is that designed for **R. van den Dorpe's** edition of 1497. Before being used by J. van Doesborgh (not later than the beginning of 1518; see L.), these cuts had passed through the hands of Hendrik Eckert, who employed them in his edition of 1512. He also used two cuts in imitation of the original set; these are found in the present edition, and one of them is No. 1 in L. See below, Nos. 31, 44. There are also two cuts (Nos. 40, 60), apparently belonging to the original set, but not mentioned by Mr. W. M. Conway ("Woodcutters of the Netherlands," pp. 314-17). I have considered a reference to his book a sufficient description, and have indicated by an asterisk those cuts which occur in the edition of 1512. It seems on the whole most probable that J. van Doesborgh inherited the set from R. van den Dorpe with his other typographical apparatus, and lent it to Eckert in 1512. Otherwise it is difficult to explain the fact that isolated cuts are found in books printed by Claes de Grave in 1517 and 1520 (not 1527), and by W. Vorsterman in 1531, at a time when they demonstrably belonged to **J. van Doesborgh.**

Other, smaller, sets are indicated by the letters B to G. Of these F and **G** alone **call for remark.** The cuts in set F are of a late date, but have **a distinctive character;** they are in the style of the middle of the sixteenth century, and shew considerable skill in the execution. Some of the cuts in set F are copies of those in the great Augsburg *Theurdanck* of 1517. Nos. 82, 90, and 91 are fairly close reproductions of those numbered 110, 12 or 25, and 29 respectively. Nos. 92, 93, 94 are close copies in reverse of 75, 100, and 108 of the *Theurdanck.* Those of set G apparently belong to an astronomical work, and are dragged in here rather promiscuously. They are also in a late style. One of these, however, No. 84, is earlier: it is found in the same state in the prognostication for 1507 printed by Adr. van Berghen (Br. Mus., MS. Harl.—Bagford fragments—5937.21). A few odd cuts remain. A large one of **Charles V.** (No. 102) was used by M. Hillenius (the publisher of this edition) in 1520. Others are taken from earlier books of our printer. Lastly, there are a few doubtful and miscellaneous cuts, which have no letter or reference attached to them, and **do not** clearly connect themselves with anything in particular.

1. Sig. **A 1 a. Block on** which are cut the first two lines of the title. 57 × 174.
2. A 1 a. Duke of Brabant on horseback under arch with 6 shields. 149 × 170.
3. A 2 b (1). = DP. title, right hand figure at top.
4. A 3 a (2). = Conway 17. 82 × 66.
*5. A 3 a (2). = Conway 20. 76 × 64.

6. A 3 b (1). Bust of a man in large cap gazing forward. [B.]
. A 4 a (2). = No. 5.
*7. A 4 b. = Conway 24. 240 × 117.
*8. B 3 b (1). = Conway 1. 74 × 63.
*9. C 1 a (1). = Conway 3. 76 × 63.
*10. C 1 b (2). = Conway 4. 86 × 64.
*11. D 1 a (1). = Conway 5. 87 × 63.
*12. D 1 b (2). = Conway 8. 88 × 67.
*13. D 3 a (1). = Conway 6. 87 × 64.
E 1 b (1). St. Alaert. = No. 12.
*14. E 4 a (1). St. Digne trampling on a dragon. ? = Conway 10. 89 × 66.
*15. E 4 b (2). = Conway 7. 75 × 62.
*16. F 1 b (1). = Conway 11. 89 × 68.
*17. F 2 b (2). = Conway 12. 90 × 68.
F 3 b (2). St. Arnout. = No. 12.
G 2 a (2). St. Mary of Oyguyes. = No. 11.
H 1 a (2). St. Ide (mother of Godfrey of Boulogne). = No. 11.
*18. H 2 b (2). St. Ide van Leeuwen. = Conway 13. 89 × 65.
*19. K 2 b (1). St. Mary killed by a spearman. = Conway 14. 89 × 66.
*20. A a 1 a. 'Nobilis Brabancia.' = Conway 23: O. No. 10.
*21. B b 1 a. = Conway 25. 180 × 139.
22. C c 2 a (1). = O. 24.
C c 2 a (2). = No. 5.
*23-28. C c 3 to D d 4. = Conway 26.
*29. E e 1 a. = Conway 38. 106 × 128.
*30. E e 2 b. = Conway 28. 108 × 131.
*31. E e 3 a (1). A copy of Conway 15 (first state). 82 × 67.
E e 3 b (1). = No. 31.
*32. F f 2 b (1). = Conway 15, second state, split. 82 × 67.
F f 4 b (1). = No. 31.
33. G g 2 a (1). A king on horseback. [C.] 95 × 66.
*34. G g 3 b. = Conway 42. 107 × 130.
*35. G g 4 a. = Conway 31. 109 × 129.
H h 1 a. = No. 34, more broken.
36. H h 2 a. = Conway 32. 108 × 132.
H h 3 a. = No. 31.
*37. H h 4 b (2). = Conway 16. 90 × 64.
J i 2 a. = No. 31.
*38. J i 4 b. = Conway 33. 109 × 132.
*39. K k 2 b. = Conway 34. 108 × 128.
*40. K k 4 b. [Not Conway 45.] In front, knights charge: others ride off to
the left [cf. Conway 39]: behind, two men seize another who is
kneeling: one brandishes a sword over him. To right of this
group are archers. 108 × 129.

79

*41. L l 2 a (2). = Conway 46, much damaged. 131 × 87.
  · L l 4 a. = No. 40.
*42. M m 1 b. = Conway 36. 109 × 128.
*43. M m 2 b. = Conway 37. 108 × 129.
  M m 3 b. = No. 29.
*44. M m 4 b. = L. 1 [an imitation of the original cuts].
45. O o 1 a (2). Half length of king with prominent nose. [D.] 39 × 37.
46. O o 3 b (2). Half length of warrior with large peacock plume. [E.]
      60 × 46.
47. O o 3 b (2). The shield of Limburg. 40 × 36.
48. O o 4 a. Horseman on caparisoned steed curvetting. [C.] 70 × 78.
49. P p 1 a (1). Beardless hook-nosed king with sword on shoulder. [D.] 39 × 36.
50. P p 1 b (2). Three-quarter length of **king** holding out large sceptre. [D.]
      37 × 30.
51. P p 2 b (1). Bust of youth **holding** sceptre: large hat, head on one **side**.
      [D.] 37 × 37.
52. P p 3 a (1). Bust of bearded man in hat and cloak: right hand held out-
      [D.] 36 × 36.
  P p. 3 b. = No. 29.
53. Q q 1 b (1). Horseman with sword and shield; horse not seen. [E.]
      58 × 58.
54. Q q 1 b (2). Fierce warrior drawing his sword. [E.] 60 × 45.
55, 56. Q q 2 b (1). Two scutcheons: the middle shields right and left **of**
      No. 20. 34 × 39, 39 × 37.
57. Q q 2 b (1). A woman holding a large arrow point downwards. 71 × 34.
*58. R r 1 b. = Conway 39. 106 × 129.
  R r 3 b. = No. 58.
  S s 2 b. = No. 58.
  S s 4 a (2). = No. 32.
  T t 1 b. = No. 29.
*59. T t 2 b. = Conway 41. 107 × 128.
*60. T t 3 b. [Not Conway 35.] A duel between two knights: the rest look
      on. Men fight on foot behind. A swordsman cuts a banner of
      the retreating force in two. On left a wooded height.
      108 × 131.
  V v 1 a (2). = No. 31.
62. V v 2 b. = Conway 40. 106 × 130.
  V v 4 a (2). = No. 54.
63. X x 1 a (1). Youth bearing the arms of France. [D ?] 35 × 28.
64. X x 4 a (1). Half length of man in mantle and a cap on one side: nose
      broken in the cut. [E.] 68 × 51.
  Y y 1 a (2). = No. 4.
*65. Y y 1 b (2). = Conway 21. 75 × 62.
  Y y 3 a (2). = No. 53.

Z z 3 a (1). = No. 46.
A A 1 b. = No. 59.
*66. A A 2 b. = Conway 43. 107 × 129.
*67. A A 4 a. = Conway 44. 104 × 130.
*68. B B 3 a. = Conway 45. One of the top corners broken off [also in 1512].
    108 × 129.
69. B B 4 b (2). A pope [curious work]. 39 × 26.
70. C C 1 a (2). Edward III., bearing the arms of England. [As No. 63.]
    35 × 27.
C C 1 a (2). = No. 63.
C C 3 a. = No. 34.
D D 1 a (1). = No. 4.
D D 2 b. = No. 68.
D D 4 b. = No. 59.
E E 4 b. = No. 29.
G G 3 a. = No. 67.
G G 4 a (1). No. 53.
71. G G 4 a (1). Shield, like Nos. 55, 56. (No shield indicated : top left in No. 20.)
72. G G 4 a (1). Another shield. (Shield shewn : top right in No. 20.)
*73. H H 1 b (2). = Conway 18. 89 × 66.
H H 2 a (2). = No. 6.
74. H H 2 a (2). Similar figure looking sideways. [B.] **30 × 30**. .
H H 4 a. = No. 67.
J J 2 a. = No. 68.
J J 4 a (1). = No. 4.
75. K K 3 a (1). One knight brandishes his sword over another prostrate. [C.]
    71 × 79.
L L 3 b. = No. 59.
M M 2 a. = No. 34.
76. M M 4 a (1). A rose.
77. M M 4 a (2). A carnation.
M M 4 a (2). = No. 31.
78. N N 2 a (2). = DP. 7. The heart is not inked in.
79. N N 3 a (1). Bust of man in cap wearing the order of the Golden Fleece.
    In the distant background is a church. [C.] 92 × 82.
*80. N N 4 b. = Conway 29. 108 × 132.
O O 4 a. = No. 62.
P P 4 a. = No. 59.
Q Q 1 a (1). = No. 45.
Q Q 2 a. = No. 62.
R R 3 a (1). = No. 70.
81. R R 3 b (1). Bust portrait of prince in furred mantle and large hat ; a coat
    of arms above his shoulder. [D.] 45 × 38.
82. S S 1 a. An execution outside the city walls. [F.] 153 × 136.

M

T T 1 a.   = No. 29.

*83. X X 2 b (1).   = Conway 19 ?   82 × 67.

84. a 2 a (2).   A comet and stars above a castle: men pointing. [Double enclosing lines. G.]

85. b 4 a (1).   = O. 250.

86. d 2 b (2).   Portrait of Mary, daughter of Duke Charles of Burgundy (b. 1457). [C ?]   69 × 49.

87. d 2 b (2).   Her arms.   46 × 41.

88. d 4 b (2).   Duke Maximilian on horseback. [C. Numerous wormholes in the block.]   98 × 67.

e 1 b.   = No. 44.

89. e 1 b.   A crown.   15 × 28.

90. e 3 b.   A man in long gown meets knight and squire riding up to the gate of a castle. [F.]   100 × 135.

91. e 4 b.   A man thrown from his horse in a hilly country. The horse performs a somersault in the air. [F.]   102 × 136.

92. f 4 a.   A knight and squire stopt at a city gate by a foot soldier. [F.]   152 × 135.

93. g 4 a.   A knight, his lady, and three attendants conversing with five burghers. [F.]   100 × 137.

94. h 1 b.   A lady, her dog, and attendants at a castle gate: a man kneeling on the steps before her. [F.]   153 × 135.

95. h 2 a.   Rude vignette of Maximilian, in a circle.   [D ?]   Diam. 38—39.

96. i 1 a.   A fierce confused battle in a hilly country. [F.]   152 × 134.

k 4 a (1).   = No. 63.

k 4 b (1).   = No. 70.

m 1 a (1).   = No. 81.

97. m 1 b.   = D P. 3.

*98. o 4 a.   = Conway 27. (Two blocks.)   109 × 63; 108 × 65.

o 4 b (2).   = No. 63.

99. p 3 a (2).   A crown with latin cross at top.   28 × 18.

p 3 a (2).   = No. 89.

100. p 3 a (2).   A beardless king on his throne: wears a hat. [D ?]   56 × 28.

101. p 4 b.   = O. 40.

102. q 1 a.   Large portrait of Charles V., with woodcut inscription.   178 × 128.

103. q 1 b (1).   The imperial eagle bearing the arms of Charles V.   86 × 67.

q 2 b.   = No. 36.

104. r 2 b (2).   = O. 191.

105. r 4 b (2).   King and his court. A dog lying in foreground. [C ?].   83 × 96.

s 4 a.   = No. 62.

106. t 4 b (1).   King of Denmark, with his arms. [D.]   45 × 37.

107. t 4 b (2).   Sceptred youth in large hat with eyes and mouth wide open. [D.]   51 × 37.

108. v 1 a (2).   King of Hungary. [As No. 63.]   34 × 28.

109. v 3 b (2).   Youth with **open** mouth; no sceptre. [D.] **52 × 37.**
110. x 1 b (1).   = L. 3.
111. x 1 b (2).   = F J. 24.
112. x 3 a (1).   The gate of a fortress, with bridge. Trees growing in **front of** it. [F.] 123 × 54.
113. **x 3 a (2).**   = N L. 19.
114. **x 3 a (2).**   Shield party per bend. Below, spirals; above, a horseman killing a man on foot. 48 × 40.
115. y 3 b (1).   = L. 2.
116. y 4 a.   Three women standing by a prostrate man. Astronomical **signs** beside each of them. [G.] 88 × 103.
117. z 2 a.   Spears, swords, stars, heads in a great flame. A hand strikes into it with a large sword. On the left, an eclipse. (?) [G.] 104 × 116.
118. z 2 b.   Bust of doctor. [B.] 28 × 37.
119. z 3 a.   Bust of student. [B.] 30 × 31.
120. z 2 b. and 3 a.   Wien besieged by the Turks. [F. ?] 167 × 219.
121. z 4 b. (2).   An old man in a cloak holding out his hands. **57 × 29.**
122. z 4 b. (2).   Woman in bed [holes and cracks in the block]. 69 × 40.
123. × 2 a.   Meeting of Pope and Kaiser, under an arch. Imperial eagle in centre. [C. ?] 119 × 119.
124. × 3 b. (2).   The left-hand figure from the top of D P. 1.
    × 4 b.   = No. 20.

30. **The** valuation **of** gold and silver.

The cuts in this book are with the exception of those on the last page all illustrations of coins, and belong to one set: they are probably identical with those used in 1500 by Liesvelt, and enumerated by Conway on p. 314. There are, however, 31 cuts, while Conway mentions 17 only. Nos. 27, 28 are found in an earlier broadside printed at the Iron Balance: see p. 37, above. Of the cuts on the last page, the upper is clearly distinguished by the interlaced branches above; the work is close and fine. It is a copy in reverse of one used at the beginning of the sixteenth century by several printers at Köln, among others by Martin von Werden in 1509, on the title of the Consolatorium Johannis de Tambaco, and in 1507 by Johann Landen. The lower cut is very rude and poor. These are quite different from any used elsewhere by J. v. Doesborgh.

1. fo. 1 a.   The Golde fleys. (*Diligite iusticiam...*)
2. —   The phus gyldon. (*S. Philipe ite...*)
3. 1 b.   The siluer flyes. (*Inicium sapientie...*)
4. —   The dowble styuer. (*Omnis spiritus...*)
5. —   The syngyle styuere. (*Sit no' domi...*)
6. 10 a.   The gyldon made at bremen...

7.	10 b.	The gyldon made at swolle...
8.	—	The gyldon made by iohn̄ Kynge ‖ of denmarke.
9.	11 a.	The gyldon made at dauentre...
10.	11 b.	The gyldon minted at dormont.
11.	—	The gyldon not long mynted by the ‖ byshop of vtrecht.
12.	12 a.	The gyldon made to wesele.
13.	12 b.	The gyldon made I y⁰ lade of ludeke.
14.	—	The gyldon made at mȳst' I westwale.
15.	13 a.	The gyldon here aforetyme whas ‖ made by **dauid of borgon** somtyme. ‖ byshop of vtrecht.
16.	13 b.	The gyldon made at emdē...
17.	—	The gyldon not long and newe ‖ made in the lande of gelder.
18.	17 b.	The good rynysh coruorster gol- ‖ dons...
		(1. Moneta nova aurea Kilen'.
19.	—	2. Moneta nova aurea Co'.
20.	—	3. Mo' aurea lipcene (?).
21.	18 a.	4. Moneta nova aur' swobac.
22.	—	5. Dated 1437.
23.	—	6. Moneta nova aurea wa.
24.	18 b.	7. As No. 5, but the lion faces the wrong way.
—		8. = No. 6.
—		9. = No. 4.
25.	—	10. Mo' Au' Rene s 1491.
26.	19 a.	11. Mone. no. francfd'.
—		12. = No. 5.)
27.	19 b.	The frenche blankes... (2 lilies, 2 crowns.)
28.	20 a.	Other frenche blankes... (4 lilies.)
29.	23 a.	The Castilian. (*Quot deus*...)
30.	—	The dobbyll docaet. (*Sub vmbra alarum*...)
31.	23 b.	The Cruysades. (*Iohanes II*... on both sides.)
32.	24 b.	Virgin and Elizabeth under canopy Infant Christ stepping between them. 79 × 60.
33.	—	Small rude cut of English **and** French arms quartered. 22 × 23.

§ 2. THE BORDERS.

Borders are used by Jan van Doesborgh chiefly for the purpose of framing in woodcut illustrations, but they are also occasionally employed to fill up a vacant space at the foot of a page or column. The borders used in FT. and PK. are undoubtedly of French origin ; the others are not distinctively French in style, and are probably of local execution. In the following list the borders are primarily arranged in chronological order by the book in which they are first found, and secondarily by the position of each in the book where it is first found.

Border 1.

Alternate rosettes, divided by a zigzag line. Two blocks, one of which (B) has
   an oblong piece broken out of one end. Both measure 56 × 9 mm.

[A.] FT. 1 a : 5 a : 5 b : 10 b : 13 b.

[B.] FT. 4 a : 9 a : 12 b.

Border 2.

Large roselike flowers, all turned in the same direction, with one leaf : each
   is divided from the other by a thin white perpendicular line. Three blocks.
   [A] measures 88 × 10 mm., and is a good deal worn, more so in PJ. than
   in FT. [B] measures 86 × 10 mm. [C] measures as [B], but is broken
   on one of the long sides.

[A]. FT. 14 b : 17 b : 21 a.

PJ. 9 a.

[B.] FT. 1 a : 14 b : 18 a : 22 b.

PJ. 4 a : 9 a : 10 a.

[C.] FT. 1 a.

Border 3.

A continuous flower and leaf pattern. The flower at one end has a broad-arrow
   mark on it. Two blocks ; [A] 75 × 10, [B] 74 × 10 mm. In all places
   except the first, B has a corner broken off. This injury is rather larger in
   PJ. than in FT.

[A.] FT. 1 a (joined to B) : 18 b (one side).

[B.] FT. 1 a : 13 b : 18 b (the other side) : 26 a.

PJ. 9 a.

85

Border 4.

Wooden stems placed zigzag: from each springs a flower, filling up the angle. There are two blocks of this, but they are not distinguishable. 90 × 11 mm.
FT. 1 b (both blocks): 8 a : 12 a : 22 b : 25 b : 26 b.

Border 5.

Foliage wreathed round a staff. On ff. 22 b, 25 a it is much worn. Measures 40 × 10 mm.
FT. 1 b : 7 b : 9 b : 22 b : 25 a.

Border 6.

Long serrated foliage in shallow curves alternately concave and convex. Measures 76 × 10 mm.
FT. 7 a : 8 b.

Border 7.

A flower pattern resembling No. 3. The flowers are star-shaped, and have five petals. Measures 43 × 11.
FT. 10 a : 11 a : 22 b : 26 a.

Border 8.

A large design in two parts. (a) Border with four dragons and a snail, separated by flowers. (b) A triple pendant, the centre having two grotesque heads. These are always used at the bottom of the page, and thick lead lines frame the other three sides. There are two blocks of (a), which has a white design on a black ground; in (a 1) the snail is at the right hand end, in (a 2) it is in the middle. Measurements: (a 1) measures at first 173 × 9; at sig. D it becomes 171-2, at sig. J it falls to 168. (a 2) is at first 170 × 10, but at sig. D becomes 167-8. (b) measures 171 × 20 in the centre. An asterisk prefixed to (a) denotes that the border is placed upside down.
This border is only found in O.

i. (a 1, b). A 1 a : C 2 a : C 4 b : D 2 b : F 1 b : F 3 a : L 1 a : L 4 a : L 6 a : M 3 b : N 4 a : Q 1 b : R 5 a : R 6 a : S 1 b : x 2 b : x 4 b : A A 2 b : P P 2 a.
ii. (*a 1, b.) B 5 b : G 3 b : G 6 b : H 2 b : J 3 a : J 5 a : K 3 a : P 1 b : G G 2 a.
iii. (a 2, b.) D 1 a : E 2 a : E 4 b : G 1 b : K 1 b : O 2 a : P 5 a : Q 2 b : Q 3 b : R 2 b : A A 1 a : C C 1 a : K K 1 a : O O 3 a.
iv. (*a 2, b.) B 3 a : I 1 a.

Border 9.

Rosettes on alternate sides, separated by a double thin white line along the centre. There appear to be several blocks of this border, not easily distinguishable: one of the corners is in some of the impressions faint, in others broken away. These are here indicated by an asterisk. Measurements in O this border measures 71 × 6-7 mm.; in FJ. and MN., 69-70; in DP. and WS. 67 only.

O. A 1 b: A 3 b: M M 2 a (1): N N 1 a (1): N N 2 a (2): N N 3 a (2): N N 4 a (2): O O 1 a (2).

FJ. 17 a.

MN. *10 b.

DP. *E 1 a (1): F 3 a (2): F 4 b (1): J 4 a (2): J 4 b (1): K 1 a (1): *L 1 a (2): *L 2 a (1): R 1 2 (1): *R 4 a (2): S 2 a (1): V 2 a (1): *X 2 a (1): Y 4 2 (2): Y 4 b (2): A a 3 a (2): H h 2 b (2).

WS. *m 4 b (2).

Border 10.

Two stems, each having four leaves springing symmetrically from each side; divided, and at each end bounded by flower-like ornaments. Measurement: in the first four books 71 × 6 mm.: in DP. first 70, then 69, and finally 67 mm.

O. A 1 b: K K 4 b: M M 2 a (1): N N 1 a (1): N N 2 a (2): N N 3 a (2): N N 4 a (2).

L. 3 b.

FJ. 18 b.

MN. 10 b.

DP. K 2 b (2): M 4 b (2): S 3 b (1).

Border 11.

Reticulated, white lines on a black ground, surmounted by a line of dog-tooth ornament. Measurement: Before DP., 70 × 6 mm.: in DP., and afterwards 68 mm.

O. A 1 b: M M 4 a: N N 1 a (2): N N 5 b (1): O O 1 a (2).

L. 3 b.

V. 25 b: 30 a.

FJ. 17 a.

DP. G 2 a (1): G 3 a (1): G 4 b (2): H 2 2 (2): J 2 a (1): J 3 a (2): K 3 a (2): M 4 b (1): R 2 a (1): S 3 b (1): V 2 a (2): Y 3 a (2).

BC. y 3 b (1).

Border 12.

A pattern of leaves or palmettes turned alternately upwards or downwards: it resembles the stereotyped representation of clouds in early woodcuts. Measurement: in O., etc., 71-2 × 7; in DP. and WS., 69 only: in BC., 66.

O.   A 1 b: A 3 b: L L 4 b: M M 4 a: N N 1 a (2): N N 5 b (1).

FJ.   18 b.

MN.   10 b.

DP.   J 3 a (1): K 3 a (2): K 4 a (2): M 1 a (2): R 1 a (2): R 1 b (1): S 3 a (1): S 3 b (1): V 1 a (2): Y 3 a (2)   Y 4 b (1): A a 2 b (1).

WS.   m 4 b (2).

BC.   y 3 b (1).

Border 13.

A large renaissance border, in four pieces. Measurement: top, 23 × 73 mm.; right side, 175 × 23; left side, 175 × 22; bottom, 30 × 73.

O.   E E 1 a (top and sides): L L 3 b (the same):
     Q Q 4 b (complete).

DP.   H h 4 b (complete).

BC.   ✗ 4 b (sides only).

Border 13a.

The bottom piece of 13, broken, and used alone. Measurement: **30 × 70 mm.**

Tdal, etc.   16 a: 16 b.

BC.   E 1 a (2): K 4 b (2): A a 4 b (2): C c 2 a (2): M m 4 a (2): t 4 a (2).

Border 13b.

A piece used to replace the top portion of No. 13. Two flat ornamental arches, with turrets between. Measurement: 13 × 106.

BC.   ✗ 4 b.

Border 14.

A border very much resembling No. 9, with the addition of a large rosette in the centre as a pendant, and an excrescence, apparently fragmentary, at each end, containing animal figures. In DP., and afterwards, these latter are broken off flush with the edge of the border itself. Measurement, 61-2 × 16-17: the end pieces are 18 mm. where perfect, 9 mm. where broken.

L.   1 b.

FJ.   1 b: 25 a.

MN.   20 a.

DP. C 1 a (1): C 1 b (2): D 3 a (2): E 2 a (1): E 3 a (2): G 1 a (2): H 1 a
(2): J 2 b (1): J 4 b (1): K 2 a (1): L 3 b (2): L 4 b (2): M 4 a (1): N 2 a
(2): N 4 b (2): Q 4 b (1): A a 4 b (2).

WS. c 2 a (2): g 4 a (2): v 3 b (1).

BC. A 4 a (2): B 4 a (2): E 1 a (2): Y y 1 a (1): Y y 3 a (2): **SS** 4 b (2):
X X 2 a (2): Z Z 1 a (2): e 1 a (2): e 3 a (2): f 3 b (2): h 1 **a (2)**: **n** 4 a
(2): **q 1 b (2)**: **s** 3 b (2): x 3 a: ✗ 1 b (2).

Border 15.

A succession of ornamental circles. There appear to be two blocks of this
border ; that occurring on fo. 20 a of MN is seemingly different from that
on fo. 1 a. Measurement : 136·7 × 10.

L. 1 b.
V. 1 a.
FJ. 1 a: 25 a.
MN. 1 a: 20 a.
DP. A a 4 b: H h 3 a.

Border 16.

A series of ovals formed by branches : at the point where the ovals join is a flower.
There are two blocks of this border, differing at one end. [A] measures 139
× 10 mm. ; [B] measures at first 137, then in DP., where one end is broken,
136 mm. On the title of FJ. this border occurs, and agrees with [B]
except in the measurement, which is 138 mm.

[A.] L. 1 b.
V. 1 a.
[B.] FJ. 25 a.
MN. 1 a, 20 a.
DP. A a 4 b: H h 3 a.
[*Doubtful.*] FJ. 1 a.

Border 17

An open-work border with three pendants. Measurement : 96 × 15 mm.
L. 3 b.

Border 18.

Architectural border in three divisions : a) a zigzag pattern : b) six ceiling panels
in perspective : c) three semicircular projections. There are at least two
blocks of this. In V. it measures 101 × 13 mm. ; in FJ., fo. 6 a, what may
be the same block measures 98 : this is the same as the one used in DP.,

where it is 97 mm. But in FJ., fo. 20 b, one end is broken off, so that it measures only 92 mm. This, therefore, cannot be the same block as that used in DP.

V. 1 a.
FJ. 6 a : 20 b.
DP. 1 b.

Border 19.

A border resembling No. 9, but on a larger scale. The line dividing the rosettes is a single thick one, and there is an outer black line attached on one of the long sides. This line is in some of the blocks thin (as used in MN., FJ., H., WS.), in others thick. There appear to be numerous different blocks of this border; but it is very difficult to distinguish them clearly. In V. only two appear to be used: No. 1 has only half a rosette at one end, while No. 2 has nearly three-quarters. In BC. this border appears in a mutilated condition.

V. [No. 1.] 7 b [left; 88 × 11-12]: 14 a [right]: 17 b [left]: 19 b.
[No. 2.] 7 b [right; 88 × 13]: 14 a [left]: 17 b [right]

FJ. 2 b [87]: 12 b [left; like 2 b, but 86 × 10]: 12 b [right; 85-6 × 12] 14 a [top; as 12 b, right]: 14 a [bottom; 87 × 10 one end, 12 the other]: 15 a [right; as 12 b, right]: 15 a [left; as 12 b, left]: 20 b [as 12 b, left]: 22 b [top; as 12 b, right]: 22 b [bottom; as 12 b, left]: 24 a [as last]: 24 a [as 12 b, right].

MN. 3 b [as FJ. 2 b; like V. No. 1, but apparently different]: 20 b [top; the same]: 20 b [bottom; 86; as FJ. 12 b, right?].

H. J 4 a [right side; broken at one end; 83 × 11]: J 4 a [left side; 85 × 10].

NL. 11 a [right; 87 × 13]: 11 a [left; 87 × 12] 24 a [right and left; apparently the same less thickly printed: 86 × 12 and 86 × 11].

WS. a 4 b [two blocks; 83, 84] k 1 b [two blocks; 82, 80]: v 3 a (2) [two blocks; 81, 84].

BC. x 1 b [two blocks; 61, 59].

Border 20.

A simple pattern of rude trefoils connected by curves; a double line below. There are many blocks of this border, which are difficult to distinguish. In V. only one block is used, measuring 64-5 mm., unless that on fo. 30 b differs from that on 30 a. In FJ. there are three blocks; [A] measuring 84 mm.; [B] originally measuring 85, but now broken in two pieces of 66 and 19 mm., and separated [B 1, B 2]; [C] measuring 63-4 mm., possibly the same as that used in V. In MN. [A] and [B] are used; the latter has its two pieces placed together. In DP. only [B 1] and [C] are found; the latter is broken, and near the end quite worn out. The example of [C] used in **NL.**, **which is** not broken, **must, unless the** book be wrongly placed after DP., be a duplicate block.

V. 17 b: 25 b: 30 a: 30 b.

FJ. [A.] 2 b: 4 a: 12 b: 18 b.
   [B 1.] 1 a: 8 b [top]: 10 b [top]: 17 a [bottom].
   [B 2.] 8 b [bottom]: 10 b [bottom]: 17 a [top]: 25 b [top].
   [C.] 8 b [bottom]: 10 b [bottom]: **17** a [top]: 25 b [top].

MN. [A.] **1 a**: 10 b.
   [B 1 and **2.**] **3 b**: **7 a.**

H. [B 1.] J 4 a.

DP. [B 1.] C 1 b (2): D 3 b (1): E 1 a (1): G 4 b (2): J 3 a (1): J 4 a (1):
   J 4 b (2): K 3 a (1): M 1 a (2): M 3 b (1): N 2 a (2): O 2 a (1) [bottom]:
   P 4 a (1): Q 4 b (2): S 2 a (2) [top]: V 1 b (1): V 4 b (1): Y 4 b (2):
   A a 1 a (1): A a 1 b (1).
   [C.] C 1 a (2): C 4 a (2): E 2 b (2): E 3 b (1): **F** 2 b (1): G 3 a (1):
   G 4 a (2): J 1 b (1): J 4 b (1): K 1 a (1) K 2 b (2): M 2 a (2): M 4 b (1):
   O 2 a (1) [top]: P 1 b (2) S 2 a (2) [bottom]: S 2 b (1): V 2 a (2): A a
   3 a (2): B b 4 a (2).

NL. [C ? *see above.*] 1 a.

WS. [A ? 81 mm.] d 2 b (1).
   [B 1.] e 1 a (2): v 3 b (1) [right].
   [C.] **e** 2 a (1): v 3 b (1) [left: 61 mm. only].

HC. [A scrap of 24 mm.] **z** 4 b (2).

Border 21.

   Two blocks always used **together,** representing ornamental renaissance half-columns, divided into two parts by a triple moulding or fillet in the centre. Measurement: 94 × 8 mm.

V. 25 b: 30 a.

FJ. 1 b: 24 b: 25 b.

MN. 20 b.

Border 22.

   A border with three pendants, very like No. 17, but smaller and less elaborate. Measurement: in FJ. 87 × 14 mm.; in MN. and H. 86; in DP. 85. There is probably more than one block.

FJ. 1 a: 1 b: 4 a: 7 a: 18 b: 24 a: 24 b: 25 a: 25 b.

MN. 1 a: 1 b: 14 b: 15 b.

H. J 4 a.

DP. 1 b.

Border 23.

The ground is white. There is a bounding line both at top and bottom. Semi-circles, inside which runs a line touching each semicircle at three points by a succession of curves. In FJ. only a scrap of this border is used, measuring 19 × 11 mm.: in **NL.** is found a larger piece, measuring 53 × 13 mm.

FJ. 8 b: 10 b.
NL. 11 a.

Border 24.

Rather to the left of the middle is a circle enclosing a rosette: on each side a renaissance ornament resembling a floriated column. Measurement: 58 × 7 mm.

FJ. 12 b.
MN. 20 a.

Border 25.

White ground. **A series** of black ovals in juxtaposition, occupying the whole breadth of the border; each oval contains two escallops placed back to back. Measurement: 147 × 10 mm. except in BC., where there is only a fragment, 53 × 10. There are two blocks.

DP. 1 b [both blocks].
NL. 1 a [**both**]: 8 b and 9 a [both].
WS. q 1 a [one only].
BC. p 3 a (2).

Border 26.

Semicircular curves, where they join **running to** a point, which is topt by a **trefoil.** From the base of each trefoil on each side to the central point of each curve **run** opposing curves: at the middle of these curves is a sort of twist. This border is open at the top, but has a bounding line at the bottom. There **are** three blocks of this border, with slightly different patterns.

[A.] measuring 67 × 13 mm., has **the twist** small, and above it **one or** more independent dots or **small** circles. **The** bounding line is prolonged perpendicularly at both ends.

[B.] measures 68 × 13 mm. The twist is larger; there are no **dots;** and there is a perpendicular bounding line at one end only.

[C.] measures 70 × 13 mm. It is like [B.], but has the bounding line at both ends.

DP. [A.] C 1 a (1): E 3 a (2): G 4 b (1): H 1 a (1) [bottom].
[B.] C 3 a (1) D 3 a (2): E 2 a (1): E 4 b (1): F 3 a (1): F 4 b (2): G 2 b (1) [bottom]: G 4 a (2): H 1 b (2) [top]: H 4 a (1): J 1 a (1) [bottom]: J 1 b (1): J 3 a (1): K 1 a (1): K 2 b (2): K 3 b (2): L 1 b (2): L 2 a (1):

L 4 b (1) [top]: M 1 a (2): M **1** b (1): M 2 a (2): N **2** b (2): O 1 a (2):
Q 1 a (2): R 1 a (1): S 1 b (1): S 3 b (1): T 1 a (1): A a 4 b [left]: B b
4 a (1): H h 2 b (1).

[C.] C 3 b (2): D 2 b (1): E 3 a (1): E 3 b (1): G 1 a (1): G 2 b (1) [top]:
H 1 a (1) [top]: H 1 b (2) [bottom]: J 1 a (1) [top]: J 2 b (2): L 3 b (2):
L 4 b (1) [bottom]: M 2 b (2): M 4 a (1): Q 4 a (1) [henceforth slightly
worn at ends; 68-69 mm.]: Q 4 b (1): R 1 b (2): S 1 b (2): S 2 b (2):
V 1 a (2): V 2 a (1): V 4 a (2): A a 4 b [right].

WS. [C.] t 2 a (2) [68 mm.]: v 3 b (2) [67 mm.].

BC. [A; with the dots cut out.] **x** 1 b [right: 65 mm.].

[B.] **x** 1 b [left].

Border 27.

A pattern **of** upturned semicircles on a black ground. Measurement:
61 × 10 mm.

DP. J 2 b (2): K **2 a** (1): L 2 a (1): L 4 b (2): M 1 b (1): M 2 b (1): N 3 a (1):
Q 1 a (2): Q 4 a (1): R 3 b (1): S 1 a (1): S 2 b (1): V 1 b (1): V 4 b (1):
X 2 a (1): Y 4 a (2): Y 4 b (1): A a 1 a (1): A a 1 b (1): H h 2 b (2).

WS. b 4 a (2): d 3 b (2): e 4 a (2).

Border 28.

Two plain pillars, one above the other, with capital and base. On one side is **a**
black strip running all along, with white spaces dug out of it. Two blocks.
Measurement: 126 × **9** mm.

WS. K 1 b [both].

BC. A a 1 a [both].

Border 29.

At ends, flowers: in centre, a bishop issuing from a flower faced by a spiral-tailed
monk. Measurement: 63 × 14 mm.

PK. 10 a: 11 a: 12 a: 19 b: 22 a.

Border 30.

Two grotesque animals, one a winged dragon passant reguardant; at ends,
flowers. Measurement: 63 × 14 mm.

PK. 10 a: 22 a: 24 a: 25 a.

Border 31.

A bold flower pattern: fleur-de-lys shaped white spaces, inside which are flowers,
divided by flowers and foliage. Measurement: 63 × 14 mm.

PK. 11 a: 12 a: 24 a.

Border 32.

Measurement · 46 × 8 mm.

PK. 13 a [right side].

Border 33.

A dragon on the left threatens a hind in the centre; on the right a flower.
Measurement 63 × 14 mm.

PK. 23 b.

Border 34.

A line of curved diamonds enclosing circles: two pieces joined in the middle. At
each end are the beginnings of the same pattern starting off at right angles.
Measurement: (78 × 77 =) 155 × 9 mm.

BC. A a 1 a [left].

Border 35.

A border formed of two different patterns joined in the middle.
(a) Diamond-shaped rosettes, the sides filled up with similar half-rosettes.
(b) Interlaced bands enclosing in succession a square, an oblong, and an oval.
Measurement: (78 × 78 =) 156 × 9 mm.

BC. A a 1 a [right].

Border 36.

As (a) of 35, with the addition of an openwork edging. Two blocks; [A] is an
end block, 41 × 15 mm.; [B] is 40 × 14 mm.

BC. M m 4 b [A, B]: N n 2 a [A]: O o 4 a [A, B]: P p 3 a (1) [A]: e 1 b
[A, B]: m 1 b [A].

Border 37.

Ovals filled with interlaced work like that of 35 (b): the intervals are filled with
fine lines. Openwork edging with an ornament in the middle. Two
blocks; [A] has a double line at both ends, [B] only at one end. Both
measure 40 × 14 mm.

BC. M m 4 b [A, B]: N n 2 a [A, B]: O o 1 a [B]: O o 4 a [A, B]: P p 1 a
[A]: P p 2 b (1) [A]: X x 1 a (2) [A, B]: N N 2 a (2) [A, B]: Q Q 1 a
(1) [A]: R R 3 a (1) [B]: R R 3 b (1) [B]: e 1 b [B]: m 1 b [A, B]
o 4 b (2) [B]: x 3 a [A, B]: y 4 a [A, B]: z 2 a [A, B].

94

Border 38.

Two double spirals (S-shaped) of Renaissance pattern joined by a band. Openwork edging with a fly in the middle. Two blocks; in B the band is black
and the fly clearer than in A. Measurement: 40 × 14.

BC. M m 4 b [A, B]: N n 2 a [B]: O o 1 a [B]: O o 4 a [A, B]: P p 1 b (2)
[A, B]: B B 4 b (2) [A, B]: N N 2 a (2) [A, B]: Q Q 1 a (1) [B]: R R
3 a (1) [B]: e 1 b [A, B]: h 2 a (2) [A, B]: k 4 a (1) [A, B]: k 4 b (1)
[A, B]: m 1 a (1) [A, B]: m 1 b [A, B]: o 4 b (2) [B]: t 4 b (1) [A, B]:
v 1 a (2) [A, B]: y 4 a [A, B]: z 2 a [A, B].

Border 39.

The same pattern as No. 34, with an openwork edging. Two blocks, both
40 × 15 mm.

BC. N n 2 a [A, B]: O o 3 b (2) [A, B]: O o 4 a [A, B]: P p 1 a (1) [A]:
P p 2 b (1) [A]: P p 3 a (1) [B]: e 1 b [B]: m 1 b [B].

Border 40.

Waisted pillar not unlike No. 21, but plain and narrower. Five blocks; [A]
measures 54 × 9 mm.; [B] 56; [C] 67; [D] 55; [E] 66.

BC. [A, B.] O o 3 b (2): Q q 1 b (2): V v 4 a (2): X x 4 a (1): Z z 3 a (1).
[B, C, D, E.] d 2 b (2).

Border 41.

A rectangular pilaster, with a circle in the middle and an abacus-like projection at
both ends. Three blocks; [A] is merely a fragment, measuring 24 × 11 mm.;
[B, C] measure 49 mm.

BC. [A.] e 1 b.
[B, C.] t 4 b (2): v 3 b (2).

§ 3. INITIALS AND ORNAMENTS.

1. LARGE INITIALS.

D. Contains figure of Moses holding the tables. 12-line. 51 × 63.
O. A 2 a.
BC. A a 1 a.
H. Black ground with white spiral pattern. 8-line. 37 × 40.
FT. 1 a.
Short accidence. 1 a.

95

I. Interlaced branches, with two men and a woman; on left, a shield bearing three fleurs-de-lys. 14-line. 65 × 49.
FT. 2 a.
J. Contains figures of two pilgrims, one standing and one kneeling. 20-line. 98 × 48.
DP. 2 a.
NL. 15 a.
WS. 2 a.
N. Contains figures of pope, cardinal, bishop, emperor, and king. 14-line. 64 × 50.
PJ. 2 a.
U. Contains a representation of the Trinity. 10-line. 47 × 48.
DP. ' O 3 a (1).

2. FRENCH INITIALS.

i. *With black ground.*

A. Flowers. 30 × 28.
BC. B 3 b (1); and nine times elsewhere.
D. Butterfly in centre. 29 × 27.
DP. A 6 a; and seven times elsewhere.
WS. K 2 b (1).
BC. A 2 a.
D. Flowers only. 28 × 27.
BC. C 1 b (2); and thrice elsewhere.
F. Belongs to a different alphabet. 32 × 32.
BC. Q Q 1 a (1).
I. With two flowers. 27 × 26.
BC. C 3 a (2); and thirty-four times elsewhere.
O. Flower in centre. 27 × 26.
BC. e 3 a (1).
V. 25 × 26.
BC. [Upside down] C 2 b (2): [do., used for A] D 3 a (1): [right] K 1 a (1).

ii. *With dotted background.*

I. With two animals. 21 × 21.
O. A 2 a : B 3 b (1): B 6 a (1).
DP. C 1 a (1).
WS. b 1 a (2).
With few exceptions, all the initials used in PK. belong to this class.

3. GROTESQUE.

An alphabet of five or six-line initials; the letters are formed by black lines of
  varying thickness; in most initials of this kind grotesque faces are introduced,
  but this is not the case with the present set.

G. BC. O o 2 a (2), and twice elsewhere.

H. WS. a 5 b, and thrice elsewhere.

  BC. H 1 a (2), and ten times elsewhere.

K. BC. q 1 b (1).

M. BC. d 3 a (1): m 1 b (1).

N. BC. T t 2 b (1): r 1 b (2).

S. BC. A 2 b (2); and four times elsewhere.

T. WS. a 3 a.

W. BC. B b 1 b (1); and twice elsewhere.

4. MISCELLANEOUS.

B. An initial once belonging to G. Leeu. 22 mm.

  WS. 1 3 a (2).

C. White on a black ground. Seven-line. 31 × 29.

  PK. 8 a.

T. A plain letter, without ground or edge lines. 27 × 27.

  WS. a 3 a (1): g 1 b (2).

5. LOMBARDIC INITIALS.

i. An A (no other letter) with inner markings and edge-line.

  FT. 19 a: 25 b.

ij. An A (no other letter) with inner markings, but no edge-line.

  FT. Seven times on and after fo. 15 a.

iij. Plain two-line initials, usually or exclusively used in all the books except
  PK., in which W only is found.

iv. One-line initials used in the text: found in FT., PJ., RL., and the Long
  accidence.

v. Very small initials used with type 2 in the large figure of Moses; O.,
  C C 3 b.

vi. Thick quasi-Lombardic three-line, I only, the upright consisting of two
  strokes.

  PJ. 4 b.

vij. A two-line E formed of thin black lines enclosing white spaces: the cross-
  stroke has diagonal black lines.

  O. M 2 b (2).

❡ ORNAMENTS.

i.   A Maltese **cross**: there are two sizes of these, and they are usually combined
     with arrangements of stops such as . · . :/:)( ):(to form a line.
     FJ. : MN. : H. : BC. (smaller cross only).

ij. A six-rayed star, 22 mm. in diameter.
     WS. q 1 a.

iij. ❧ This is used very frequently in BC., chiefly in combination with iv., at
     the sides of the cuts in the Chronicle **set**. The greatest number found **on**
     one page is 44 on E e 1 a and G g 4 a.

iv. ✗ Used chiefly in combination with iij., but also as a signature at the end of
     BC. The greatest number on any one page is 28 **on** T t 1 b and C C 3 a.

v.   A trefoil ornament resembling a piece of border 20 cut off. Used only in
     BC. Two are found on O o 3 b (2) and Q q 1 b (2); four on X x 4 a (1)
     and Z z 3 a (1). This ornament is found on the title of the Dutch *Virgilius*
     printed by W. Vorsterman.

ADDITIONS AND CORRECTIONS.

P. 5. *The Iron Balance.* The following extract from the *Historisch Onderzoek naer den oorsprong . . . der openbare plaetsen . . . , van de stad Antwerpen*, Antw. 1828, p. 107, throws light on this address: " Yzer Waeg. Op den hoek van de zoogenaemde Luizenmarkt, en van de Yzeren Waeg is een huis, de Yzeren Waghe, dat de stad toebehoorde." The plan by P. Verbiest shews the Luizenmarkt as a street turning out of the Steenhouwers Veste, a prolongation westward of the Lombaerde Veste ; it ran almost parallel to the Cammerstraet. The *Yzeren Waeg* was a small open space on the eastern side some distance along, and the house so called was at the corner of this place and the Luizenmarkt.

P. 5. *Inden aren van die vier evangelisten.* The meaning of the word *aren* seems doubtful. I owe to the kindness of a friend the suggestion that it = eren, the French *aire*, here ' an open space,' and that the place meant was the crossways formed by an intersecting street halfway up the Lombaerde Veste, where the signs of " The Eagle " and of " S. Mark " still remain.

P. 32. Another copy of the *Dieren Palleys* was sold at the Enschedé sale in 1867 (sale catalogue, No. 890). A long description of this book is given by **C. G. Hultman,** *Bibliographische Zeltzaamheden*, 1818, 8°, pp. 7, *199.*

P. 35, No. 26. Two leaves (sig. B) of an edition of the *Parson* in low German verse printed at Lübeck about 1500 by M. Brandiss or S. Arndes are in the British Museum [C. 18. e. 1 (45)]. They probably belong to the same edition as the Berlin fragment. There are two woodcuts, the second of which is clearly the **original** of No. 2 in **the** English edition.

P. 36, **No.** 29. Another copy of the *Cronike van Brabant,* wanting sheets D d and M M, is described by Mr. G. D. Bom in *Bibliotheca Belgica,* "*Vlaemsche Druckers*" *1526 tot 1599*, Amst. 1894, 4°; p. 11, No. **13.**

P. 45, No. 12. A book entitled " Een wandelinghe der kersten menschen mit Jhesu den brudegam der sielen inden hof der bloemen," printed at Amsterdam 18 Dec. 1506, contains a number of cuts which are either closely copied from the *Oorspronck* set C, or are the originals of that set. They differ only in minute details. Cuts corresponding to Nos. 77, 89, 94, 101, **103,** 106, 109, 116, 117, 119, 122, 125, 139, 227 of the *Oorspronck* are there found.

P. **73.** *Wonderful Shape.* No. 109 is a mistake, and is to **be struck out.**

LIST OF PLATES.

O s mouth a face a chyne a tote anote a a tonge   roffe of the mouth.

O s facies mentū de no guttur lingua palatū
a bade   absowe   a bye a forhede teples a lyppe

Barba super cilium ciliū frons tēpora labiū
an eye bote   anye the   fye the the whyt of the eye apple of the eye.

Palpebra sic oculus acies albugo   pupilla
the typ of the nose. fmyuel of the nose. the space bet wene the nose thyrlio

Pirula   puo nasi funt inter finia naris
of the bode brampan   a toppe a de tuydyng of the bere   a nere

Et capitis trinum vertex discrimen   et auris
the fortop part. the mydde part. the hynder part of the bede. brayne.   a parte

Sinciput ast interciput occiput   et cerebrū ys
a chyce   a gome   a forhede   an here.

Faux et iungiua cum fortilla capilus
a gryftell   a dew lap   a grethe to the

Est cartilago sic legia sic genuinus
palme of the hande. wynt handes   an belbow   brawen of the arme

Palma   iunetture manibus sūt vlna lacertus
fopleo   fyngyro a fholder   a bicft   a neck

Vngues cū digitis hume rus cū pectore collus
armepyt a fyft   a cubyt   bloode   a let

Acelle pugnus cubitus cum sanguine manus
a belly   a blodder   a bac   a backbone   a rybbe

Venter vesica tergum spondilia costa
a nauell   a fyde   fiesthe. skyn. borodypo

Est vmbilicus latus et caro pelle nates funt
a berte. a melt. a long.   a splene. a gal. a mydrsf. a maw. the rem of the bat

Cor splen pulmo lien fel ren diafragma iecur
wynd pipis a stomake   bowelles   a mawe.

Arterie stomachus post intestina sic e par
an ars   a thygh yong beer. a back   a backbone   the ende of the gut

Anus crus pubes dorsum sic spina poderqz
whyel boue   knyes   the kneknap   a fenow

Vertebra cum genibus sum internodia neruus
an būme   fhyne the fkyne of concepcyon   ankyll

Poples atqz sura matrix sic addito area.
brawne of the arme.   a veyne. leege   the master veyne

Musculus   ꝧ vena tibia sic atqz sophena
a too   the foolof the fote an bele   mary   an anklay

Articulus planta cum calce medulla cauilla
an bele   a pothe

us dicetur semita callis

PLATE I.

PLATE II.

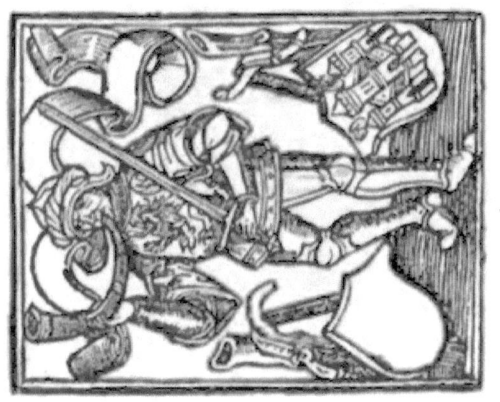

PLATE. III.

Ere beginneth a lytel trea
tyse the whiche speketh of
the xv. tokens the whiche
shullen bee shewed afore ye
dredfull daye of Jugement.
And who that oure lorde
sh all aske rekenyng of eue.
ry body of his wordis wot
dis and thoughtes. And who oure lorde wyll she.
we. vs other xv. tokens. of his passion to theym
that been depeth in dedely synne.

PLATE V.

PLATE VI.

PLATE VII.

⸿ The Coppe of the letter how ŷ
the moste meruelous and wōder
full felde was foghten / whiche of
late harþe bene sene in the londe
of Bergame..

⸿ Also ŷ copp of ŷ letter ŷ ŷ grete
Turke sent to our holy fader the
Pope.

PLATE VIII.

PLATE IX.

¶ Of the newe lādes and of ꝑ people founde by the messengers of the kynge of portyngale named Emanuel.

Of the .x. dyuers nacyons crystened.

Of pope Johñ and his landes and of the costely kepes and wonders molodyes that in that lande is.

PLATE X.

PLATE XII.

CHISWICK PRESS :—CHARLES WHITTINGHAM AND CO.
TOOKS COURT, CHANCERY LANE, LONDON.

www.ingramcontent.com/pod-product-compliance
Lightning Source LLC
Chambersburg PA
CBHW020753020726
47495CB00008B/2405